She rubbed her palms on her pants, then fisted her hands so that her nails dug into her flesh. The sensation was a touchstone to help get her mind off the absurd possibility that there had been a double meaning in what Miles had said.

You know there was. It was as palpable as her rapid heartbeat.

It was the way he'd said it, and despite the little voice inside her head that warned that she was playing with fire, that *now* of all times was not the time to get distracted by physical attraction. Because she was already preoccupied with the possibility of moving back to St. Michel—and she'd told him her secret even before she'd told her best friends and coworkers....

Still, despite good sense and propriety, she heard herself saying to him, "You want to see more of me? Is that strictly professional...or personal?"

"Both," he said.

Dear Reader,

Sometimes characters live within other stories in a series for a while before they get their own book. That was the case with Sydney James, the heroine of *Celebration's Bride.* Sydney patiently played a supporting role in four books before being cast as the heroine of this story.

She first appeared in *Accidental Princess,* where she lost at love but won three best friends. The four would eventually go on to form Celebrations, Inc., catering company and eventually star in their own television show about the inner workings of the catering business. Sydney was always content to live in the background while her friends shined. Then she met hero Miles Mercer and not only did he make her see it was *her* time to shine, he helped her realize that sometimes love and "family" are in the most unexpected places.

I hope you'll love reading Sydney and Miles's love story as much as I loved writing it. Please let me know what you think. You can reach me at nrobardsthompson@yahoo.com.

Warmly,

Nancy

CELEBRATION'S BRIDE

NANCY ROBARDS THOMPSON

HHARLEQUIN® SPECIAL EDITION®

ISBN-13: 978-0-373-65755-1

CELEBRATION'S BRIDE

Books by Nancy Robards Thompson

Harlequin Special Edition

†*Fortune's Unexpected Groom* #2185
**Texas Wedding #2214
**Texas Magic #2218
**Texas Christmas #2224
***Celebration's Bride* #2273

Silhouette Special Edition

Accidental Princess #1931
Accidental Cinderella #2002
*The Family They Chose #2026
Accidental Father #2055
Accidental Heiress #2082

Harlequin NEXT

Out with the Old, In with the New
What Happens in Paris (Stays in Paris?)
Sisters
True Confessions of the Stratford Park PTA
Like Mother, Like Daughter (But in a Good Way)
  "*Becoming My Mother…*"
Beauty Shop Tales
An Angel in Provence

*The Baby Chase
†The Fortunes of Texas:
   Whirlwind Romance
**Celebrations, Inc.

Other titles by this author
available in ebook format.

NANCY ROBARDS THOMPSON

Award-winning author Nancy Robards Thompson is a sister, wife and mother who has lived the majority of her life south of the Mason-Dixon line. As the oldest sibling, she reveled in her ability to make her brother laugh at inappropriate moments, and she soon learned she could get away with it by proclaiming, "What? I wasn't doing anything." It's no wonder that upon graduating from college with a degree in journalism, she discovered that reporting "just the facts" bored her silly. Since she hung up her press pass to write novels full-time, critics have deemed her books "funny, smart and observant." She loves chocolate, champagne, cats and art (though not necessarily in that order). When she's not writing, she enjoys spending time with her family, reading, hiking and doing yoga.

Dedication:

This book is dedicated to Gail Chasan for all you do.

Acknowledgment:

Special thanks to Caroline Phipps
for her continued help with all things army-related.

Prologue

"Did you tell *anyone* you were coming to St. Michel?" Maya LeBlanc asked.

As she watched Sydney James shake her head, she wondered how such a smart, capable, beautiful woman could be so clueless about everything that was good and right for herself.

"Nobody in Celebration, Texas, knows I'm here," Sydney said. Her British accent sounded so crisp and proper. "I don't want to say anything until I know whether or not I have the position. There is no sense in getting everyone up in arms if I'm not chosen for the job."

Sydney shrugged.

Maya sensed hesitancy in the usually self-possessed woman.

"So this is not what you want, then?" Maya asked as she stirred the pot of drinking chocolate she was preparing for the two of them.

Sydney did a double take. Her narrowed gaze flitted from Maya's face to the copper pot of chocolate, then back to Maya.

"I'm not sure I understand what you mean," she said. "Of course I would love a cup of chocolate, if that's what you're asking."

Maya put her free hand on her hip and studied Sydney. "I'm talking about the job interview. You've made the process so clandestine. I don't understand why you're keeping it from everyone who cares about you. If moving back to St. Michel will truly make you happy, then it shouldn't be such a secret."

Maya watched Sydney's body language intently as the woman studied her hands, shifting from one Ferragamo-clad foot to the other. She swallowed hard before she cleared her throat.

"It's time for me to leave Texas," she said. "It's time to move on. That's all."

Right. Maya's friend sounded as excited as a woman who was marching to her death.

"Why couldn't you tell A.J., Pepper and Caroline?" Maya asked. "Your friends would be happy for you. They wouldn't hold you back if this were truly your path. Unless you don't really want to leave?"

Sydney didn't answer.

Maya averted her gaze to the bubbles in the chocolate and quickened the pace with which she stirred. She grabbed a pinch of cinnamon and dropped it into the pot. Its coppery, sienna color stood out against the dark, rich brown of the chocolate, forming a rough design that made Maya do a double take.

Interesting...

She watched the image shift as the liquid boiled. She never knew when or how *the sign* would present itself. Sometimes the message came on the wind, other times—like now—it registered itself randomly, as it seemed to be doing in the chocolate. There was no way to predict it. But when it turned up it was unmistakable.

Maya's breath caught and her heartbeat quickened as she stole a glance at Sydney, whose sad eyes revealed more than Maya was sure Sydney wanted to tell.

Maya just needed to be sure this was indeed the sign. So she added a small pinch of cayenne pepper to the pot.

And there it was. As plain as if someone had handed her an engraved note.

Sydney was *next.* She was the *intended.*

The realization sent shivers of delight skittering through Maya. In addition to being a third-generation *chocolatier,* Maya was *un marieur.* A matchmaker. It was an avocation of sorts.... She would confess it really was her passion. Making and selling chocolate put food on her table, but bringing soul mates together fed her soul.

"Why is your heart set on leaving Texas?" Maya asked as she removed the pot from the flame.

"I get this way every so often," Sydney said. "I must have a bit of gypsy in me because sometimes the urge to move on to somewhere new is consuming."

Sydney sounded more sure of herself than she had

before, but Maya still detected the false bravado hiding beneath the polished veneer. "It's the same restlessness that drew me away from St. Michel to Texas."

"And now you want to come back to St. Michel?" Maya raised a brow at her friend as she carefully poured the thick liquid from the shiny copper pot into two demitasse cups. "As I recall, there was a man involved when you moved last time. Is that the case now?"

"No. All I've done since I've been in Celebration is work. I haven't had time for a man. That's part of the reason I want to move on."

Maya studied the jars of special herbal mixtures on the shelf above her head. She sensed that all-work-and-no-play Sydney just might need a *little something* to wake her up. Something to help her recognize that opportunity might not necessarily come calling in the form of a job offer from the Royal House of Founteneau.

Maya had a gut feeling the *opportunity* that *the sign* foretold would present itself in a much sexier manifestation. But Sydney needed to slow down, to light in one place long enough to give her future time to take root.

Maya didn't make this stuff up. She was simply the messenger. And it was clear to this courier that she had a life-changing message to deliver.

She pushed the small cup across the marble counter to Sydney, who accepted it with a grateful smile.

"Mon amie," Maya said, her cup poised midair just before her first sip. "What are you running from?"

Sydney sampled the drink. Maya glimpsed a thoughtful look in her friend's green eyes a split second before she closed them to savor the treat. When Sydney opened her eyes, she said, "I'm not running from anything."

She smiled and tilted her head ever so slightly to the right. If Maya didn't know better, she might've been fooled by her friend's resolute facade. She wasn't about to let her get away with this charade.

"Then what are you running *to?*" Maya asked.

A little laugh escaped Sydney and her fingers fluttered to her lips. "What is that supposed to mean?"

Maya took down a glass plate from a shelf behind the counter. "So you answer my question with a question?" She filled the plate with several truffles and chocolate-dipped Madeleines, specialties of the house. "If you're not running from something, that must mean you are running *to* something."

Sydney wrinkled her nose. "No, I'm not doing that, either." She set her cup on the counter and crossed her arms over her middle. Maya recognized the defensive body language for what it was. However, if the young woman hadn't wanted her help, then she wouldn't have come into the shop so eager to share the details of the job prospect that she was taking such great pains to hide from those closest to her. Maya owed it to Sydney to give her the advice she sought. Even if her friend didn't seem to like the answer or seem consciously aware that she was seeking counsel.

"*Au contraire, mon amie.* How will you ever meet your soul mate if you don't stay in one place long enough to unpack?" Maya set the plate of sweets in front of Sydney. "I am afraid what I have to say isn't what you want to hear. However, I implore you. It will be a grave mistake if you leave Celebration, Texas, now. Because your soul mate will arrive soon looking for you."

Chapter One

It was going to be one of *those* days. Sydney James could already tell. Her return flight from St. Michel to Texas, after her whirlwind trip to interview for the job of press secretary to St. Michel's royal family, had been delayed six hours. Three hours in the terminal and three hours stuck on the runway.

Much of that time had been the middle of the night in Texas, and a good portion had been spent in the air where she couldn't use her cell phone, anyway. All she'd been able to do was leave a message that she was going to be late for work—several hours late.

She'd been vague about her plans for the weekend, opting not to tell anyone about the job interview until she had a better handle on whether she even wanted the position. And, of course, whether the job wanted her. For that reason, she'd never been happier to talk to a voice mailbox. Voice mailboxes didn't hammer her with questions.

Thursday, when she'd left Texas, she'd driven herself to the airport and left her car in long-term parking so she wouldn't have to bother anyone for a ride to and from Dallas/Fort Worth International. Once she was back on Texas soil, she'd rushed to her car to get back to the office. Now she sat parked in front of Celebrations, Inc., Catering Company. Before she went in, she needed to catch her breath and make herself presentable. Running on little sleep for the better part of the past twenty-four hours, she looked like hell. She studied her reflection in her compact mirror. She had dark circles under her eyes, which made her irises look a peculiar shade of olive rather than their usual medium green, and her face looked drawn and pale. She reapplied powder, blush and lipstick with the silent prayer that maybe, just maybe, she could make herself look halfway human.

Fat chance, she thought as she snapped the compact closed. The camera never lied.

Since it was already noon and she'd missed her call time by several hours, she hoped they'd greet her with the news that they needed time to regroup and wanted to reschedule the scenes she was in for tomorrow—or better yet, later in the week. Or best-case scenario, maybe they hadn't missed her at all and had taped without her.

Yeah, right.

She knew that was a bad attitude. How many women would love to have her spot on *Catering to Dallas,* a reality TV show that chronicled the inner workings of Celebrations, Inc., Catering Company? She'd never been the center of attention on the show, and she preferred it that way. Content to carry out her duties as the catering company's public relations director, staying in the background as her three friends and co-stars Pepper Merriweather-Macintyre, A.J. Sherwood-Antonelli-Harrison and Caroline Coopersmith-Montgomery vied for the spotlight.

Sydney slipped her cosmetics back into the inner pocket of her handbag and let herself out of the car.

"Here goes," she murmured under her breath, willing there to be a fresh pot of coffee on the craft-services table.

She slipped inside the back door into the kitchen and glanced around. The white cabinets and gold-and-brown solarius granite looked fresh and clean. An array of vegetables befitting a farmers' market was artfully arranged on the center island. The area was obviously ready for a shoot. However, everyone seemed to be on a break. At least they weren't in the middle of taping. Although, if they had been, there would've been someone stationed outside the door to keep her from wandering into the shot.

"There you are." Sydney jumped as Pepper seemed to appear behind her from out of nowhere. To be caught that unawares, Sydney must have been more exhausted than she realized.

She put a hand on her chest. "You nearly gave me a heart attack."

"I'm sorry," Pepper said, her Southern accent thicker

than usual as she bit off the words. "But where on earth have you been? We've had quite a bit of excitement on the set this morning. Didn't you get my messages? I've been trying to call you."

Sydney hadn't. Her phone was tucked inside her purse, still on airplane mode. She rifled through her handbag until she found her cellular, her fingers first finding her keys, a travel-size bottle of hand sanitizer and the small bag of pretzels they'd given her on the plane before she located what she was looking for. She pulled it out and changed the setting. More than a dozen calls and texts blew up her phone.

As director of public relations, she was rarely out of touch. She gave the messages a cursory glance before dropping her phone back into her purse and returning the bag to her shoulder. Most of the messages were from Pepper. She would deal with the other texts and voice mails later. As she braced herself for Pepper's inquisition, she wondered if subconsciously she'd forgotten to turn on her phone to avoid questions about her absence before it was absolutely unavoidable.

And that time was now. Better to head off the questions by volunteering information.

"I had to go out of town this weekend and my return flight was delayed."

"You what?" Pepper asked. "Where'd you go? Why didn't you tell anyone?"

Sydney waved off the question as if it were no big deal. "Long story. But tell me, what's happening here?"

Just as Sydney hoped, Pepper lost the scent of her own inquiry and pounced on the decoy.

"Oh. My. Gosh. You won't believe it." Her voice was a hushed stage whisper. She looked around as if worried someone might overhear her. "Bill Hines had to take a personal leave of absence. We walked in this morning to find out that we have a brand-new director. At least for the time being."

Pepper pointed with her nose toward the other side of the large kitchen. Sure enough, there stood a tall, dark haired, broad-shouldered man talking to the executive producer, Aiden Woods. Sydney couldn't tell what he looked like because she could only see his profile. The men stood behind the set lights. The new guy's features were somewhat cloaked in shadows.

"Don't let his good looks fool you," Pepper said. "The guy's a slave driver of the worst kind."

For some reason, maybe it was the lack of sleep, Pepper's melodramatics struck Sydney as funny. A small hiccup-laugh escaped.

"Right. You laugh now, but just wait," Pepper warned. "He was not too pleased with you this morning when you missed your call time."

"What?" Sydney asked, suddenly sobered by the news that she might be in trouble. "I didn't have a call time." Yes she did. "Well, not an individual spotlight, anyway."

Pepper put up her hands. "Hey, don't shoot the carrier pigeon. I am just giving you fair warning."

Now that the news had had a chance to sink in, Sydney found herself getting a tad irritated. This guy comes in unannounced and takes roll? No. They weren't used to *checking in,* and as far as she was concerned, they weren't going to start now. Who did he think he was, coming in and shaking up a system that worked just fine?

"Why didn't he just shoot the scene without me?" Sydney asked.

"He did. Sort of. *Ooh,* come here. Let's go find A.J. and Caroline. They're hiding in your office."

Sydney stole one more glance at the new director. "Is he really that bad?"

Pepper grimaced and grabbed Sydney by the hand, all but dragging her the long way through the building, via the front reception area, circumventing the new guy, Aiden and the rest of the crew.

"Who the hell is he, anyway? And who does he think he is, coming in here with an attitude?"

Pepper didn't answer. Their friends weren't in the office but had ventured out to the craft-services table, which was tucked into an out-of-the-way alcove in the back of the Celebrations, Inc., Catering Company shop.

"Look who I found." Pepper was still using that absurd stage whisper.

A.J. and Caroline took it one step worse. They pantomimed a mixture of shock and relief. What? Were they no longer allowed to speak at a normal decibel? They whisked Sydney into the office and shut the door.

"Oh, my dear God," said A.J., finally using normal volume. "Where have you been?"

A.J. raked her hands through her hair, looking panic-stricken. That was when Sydney realized something was very wrong. Pepper might be the resident drama queen, but A.J. was calm, cool and levelheaded. Usually, Sydney envied her composure. When A.J. flapped, there was reason to be concerned.

"That doesn't matter. I'm here now. Please fill me in on what's going on."

A.J. explained how Aiden had said Bill Hines had a family emergency and had introduced Miles Mercer as the new interim director.

"Miles Mercer…?" Sydney repeated. "Where do I know that name from?"

"Come here." Caroline motioned Sydney to come behind the desk. She typed something into the computer's internet browser. A long list of hits came up for…Miles Mercer. When Sydney saw the thumbnail of the *Past Midnight* movie poster, the pieces began to fall into place.

That Miles Mercer.

She'd heard of him and his scary movie, *Past Midnight,* a low-budget horror flick. Everyone had heard of him. Not only was he a local boy who'd made good, but a few years ago, the movie had been a runaway box-office sensation, and was declared a cutting-edge approach to filmmaking.

What the heck was he doing here on the set of *Catering to Dallas?*

"Really?" She pointed toward the door. "That's him?"

"Yes," said A.J. "Apparently, he's a good buddy of Aiden's and flew in immediately after Bill asked for leave."

"Do you know he's only twenty-nine years old?" Pepper asked. Even though her expression was disapproving, her eyes were large and held that certain awed reverence reserved for only the most gorgeous men. "Bless his heart, but that's too young to have been called a genius. Don't you think?"

Sydney commandeered the mouse and clicked on the first *Miles Mercer* listing on the browser page—one of those "e-encyclopedia" sites that offered comprehensive morsels of info in easily digestible bites. She quickly read what it had to report about him.

Yes, he had apparently been heralded a genius among the Hollywood types for his *innovative* movie-making style. It also noted that he'd made *Past Midnight* when he was in college. He'd entered it in various contests and film festivals, and it morphed into an overnight box-office success.

Sydney hadn't seen the movie or any of the films he'd made since. The "e-encyclopedia" pointed out that none of his later projects had scored the rave reviews or box-office success of *Past Midnight*. Sydney was un-impressed; even if *Past Midnight* was groundbreaking, horror was not her favorite genre. Who wanted to be scared out of her wits and uncomfortable being alone in her own home?

As she stared at the framed Audrey Hepburn poster on her office wall, she heard herself make a disapprov-ing noise that she hadn't meant to be audible.

"If he's such a big shot, what in the world is he doing on the set of *Catering to Dallas?*" She looked up from the computer to see her friends staring at her, and for a moment she was afraid she had insulted them.

"I mean no offense. I'm part of this cast, too. It's just

that Celebration, Texas, isn't Hollywood and as much as we'd like to think our show is a pop-culture phenomenon, it's reality TV. It is what it is and it certainly isn't *cutting edge.*"

The girls shrugged and murmured that she did have a point. They also suggested that the sooner Sydney introduced herself to Miles and faced whatever wrath he might have in store for her, the better. They were only supposed to have taken a fifteen-minute break, during which he was going to go over some notes with Aiden, and then they were supposed to get back to work.

Caroline sighed. "If we don't get out there, he's probably going to come looking for us. That's just how he is. You'll see."

"Why do I feel as if I'm on my way to the principal's office for a reprimand?" Sydney asked as they all filed out of the office and made their way back to the craft-services area, where they came to a halt when they realized that Miles was still on the other side of the kitchen, still deep in conversation with Aiden.

If she positioned herself just right in the craft-services nook, she could steal glances at the infamous Miles Mercer without him being the wiser. At this angle his face was turned toward her and was no longer cloaked in shadows as it had been when she first saw him.

The "e-encyclopedia" reconnaissance mission had painted an interesting picture of their new interim boss and the pictures had proven that he was a nice-enough-looking guy, but what the research hadn't done was prepare Sydney for how drop-dead gorgeous Miles Mercer actually was in person. The photos hadn't done him justice.

Unwittingly, Sydney found herself doing the math in her head: he was five years her junior. Her gaze took a leisurely walk down the length of him, taking advantage of this moment when she could drink him in and size him up before she would be subjected to *his* scrutiny.

He was tall, dark and broad-shouldered. His hair was thick and cut in one of those effortlessly hip styles— not really long, but too long to be considered short. It was slightly curly and stood up a little on top, as if he'd rolled out of bed and carelessly combed it with his fingers. He was clean-shaven, and wore jeans and a long-sleeved black T-shirt.

If her friends hadn't warned her that he had such a disagreeable disposition, things might be looking sort of…*delicious* in the Celebrations, Inc., kitchen. *"Mmm-mmm-mmm."* Pepper smacked her lips as she poured herself a mug of coffee. "With his temper, I'll bet he's hell on a Triscuit in bed."

A.J. and Sydney laughed. Caroline nearly choked on the bite of bagel she was chewing. Once she'd recovered, she shot Pepper a pointed look.

"What?" Pepper drawled. *"Come on.* He's a good-looking guy. Everything aside, you have to give him that. I may be married, but I can still look. And appreciate."

Pepper had just come back to the show after a brief hiatus to deal with personal issues of her own. Last year had been a series of ups and downs for her and her family. On one hand, she'd met and married the love of

her life, Rob Macintyre. But she'd also
Star Energy, the company her father h
empire, implode under a criminal inves
her father had ultimately suffered a heart attack and
passed away before he could go to trial.

Pepper had confided that in her heart she would always believe her father was innocent. Sydney, A.J. and
Caroline were all glad to have her back on the show and
at Celebrations, Inc., where she had an opportunity for
a fresh start. That was part of the reason that Sydney
was so ambivalent about telling her friends she was
thinking of leaving the show. She and Pepper shared
a lot of the same duties. Where Sydney's official title
was public relations director, they all called Pepper the
company's "social connector" because of the incredible
social "ins" she possessed that only a Texas debutante
could bring to the table.

Before landing the show *Catering to Dallas,* they'd
started Celebrations, Inc., Catering Company, which
had been A.J.'s brainchild. During that time, Pepper had
lived a cushy lifestyle. Money was the furthest thing
from her mind. She came and went as she pleased,
bringing in new clients and leaving the bulk of the PR
and marketing work to Sydney. She didn't draw a salary.

Sadly, last year, her financial situation had taken a
turn for the worse as a result of the investigation in-
volving her father's company. Pepper had no part in
the scandal, of course, but she had been left holding the
bag. Sydney admired the way she'd managed to put her
life back together. She'd married a man who had more
money than the royal family of St. Michel, but she re-

...ained adamant about making her own money. If the crisis had taught her one thing, it was from that day forward, she would make her own way in the world, depending on no one. Not even her husband's fortune.

She had insisted on distancing herself from *Catering to Dallas,* so not to taint the show with her family's bad reputation. Now that everything had settled, Pepper was back. What better way for her to carve out her own place in this world than by taking over the reins of PR for the catering company and reality television show? Especially since the possibility of Sydney getting the St. Michel press secretary position was very strong.

Pepper's life was in Texas. Sydney wanted to travel. Really, it was time for her to move on. She'd been in Celebration long enough. She had never been comfortable staying in one place too long.

As activity continued to swirl on and around the set in preparation for the next shoot, which, according to A.J., would feature all four of the women in the office and kitchen discussing menus for upcoming events, Sydney continued to study Miles...until, suddenly, as if he'd sensed someone looking at him, Miles glanced in Sydney's direction. Their gazes locked.

He cocked a brow and smiled.

Sydney couldn't decide if it was genuine or a so-glad-you-could-join-us look.

Okay. So here we go.

She steeled herself and smiled back at him, forcing warmth into her eyes and refusing to be the one to look away first—even when the voice in her head said, *Heavens, he is gorgeous.*

Holding her gaze, he said something to Aiden, who slanted her a quick glance. Both men started walking toward the craft-services area.

"Oh. Here he comes," Caroline whispered.

"Good afternoon, Sydney," said Aiden. "I'd like to introduce you to your new director. This is Miles Mercer. You'll be working with him until Bill comes back. I'm guessing that by now you've heard that Bill is out?"

"Yes, Pepper brought me up to speed on everything."

"Good," said Aiden. "Miles, this is Sydney James."

"Hello, Sydney," Miles said. "It's nice to meet you." He offered his hand and she accepted it, giving a firm but feminine squeeze. Their gazes locked again—and if Sydney hadn't known better, hadn't been forewarned that he was mad as hell at her for being late—she might have imagined that something sensuous had just passed between them because for a split second, it seemed as if they were the only two in the room.

To break the awkward moment, words just started spilling out of Sydney's mouth. "We're so happy to have you with us, Miles. I would imagine they keep you pretty busy over on the West Coast. I was surprised when I learned that you were willing to take a break and come work with us—and on such short notice, too. How in the world did Aiden tempt you away from Hollywood to come to Celebration, Texas? It must be somewhat of a culture shock for you."

Miles shook his head. "Actually, I grew up in Celebration, but it's been ages since I've been back. It's nice to have the opportunity to come home and visit my family."

A-ha. That's why. It made sense.

"We're all from Celebration," Pepper volunteered hesitantly. "Well, except for Sydney. She's our British import, but we love her like a sister. I suppose we've never met before this because we were a few years ahead of you in school."

His gaze was back on Sydney as if he hadn't heard Pepper's comment. "I thought I detected an accent. When did you come across the pond? Or do they still say that?"

He smiled and she noticed that he had the slightest gap between his two front teeth. Just enough of an imperfection on an otherwise-perfect face to make her sigh inwardly.

Then she realized he was actually waiting for her to answer. "Of course we still say across the pond. No worries."

Well, no worries for *him.* She, on the other hand, was trying to play it cooler than she felt. She was such a bad actress. It was a good thing she simply had to be herself on the set. Even so, she needed to center herself as quickly as possible. To do that, she reminded herself that no matter how dark and interesting Miles was, technically he was her boss. At least for the interim. She needed to maintain a modicum of professionalism, especially since she'd already made a bad first impression by being late.

"Well, we're behind schedule," Miles said. "We should get back to work. Ladies, Debbie has the shooting updates. Why don't you go take a look?"

He nodded at A.J., Pepper and Caroline. Sydney

knew the unspoken message was for them to get lost for a moment. And they did just that.

"We'll start in five," he called over his shoulder.

As soon as they were out of earshot, he said, "We missed you this morning. Was there an emergency?"

At least he had the good grace not to reprimand her in front of the others. Actually, his tone was quite professional…nice, even. Not at all what she expected after the monstrous buildup her friends had given him. Maybe he wasn't a morning person? A grouch until the caffeine was coursing through his veins? Whatever the explanation, Sydney was grateful for his civilized manner.

"I was out of town this weekend and my return flight was delayed. I apologize if I inconvenienced anyone."

He nodded, letting the pregnant silence hang between them for a moment.

"I'm glad it was nothing serious. We're all professionals and from here on out, I'm confident you will be on time and ready to work when you're scheduled."

She might have been tempted to challenge him, or at least defend herself because normally she was on time. However, there was something about the way his sexy gaze bore into her in silent expectation that gave her a strange sense of déjà vu.

Chapter Two

If Miles had had any trepidation about coming back to Texas, the risk was certainly worth the reward, he thought as he made a concerted effort to keep his eyes from wandering back to Sydney James.

She was sitting in a director-style chair, getting her hair and makeup touched up—last looks—before they began shooting.

He walked over to the coffeepot, helped himself to a cup and stood back. He wanted to get a feel for how the cast members interacted without the glare of the lights and the intimidation of the camera.

Now that he'd met Sydney, he got the same vibe from her in person that he'd gotten as he'd watched the dailies from recent shoots and footage from the first season. His instincts were right. She looked as fabulous in person as she had on screen.

Even though he was only here for a short time, he was considering spotlighting her a little more by working in an interesting story line that featured her, but he needed to figure out how to best do that before he announced this plan to the rest of the cast.

He needed to gather his thoughts before they resumed shooting. Aiden had asked him to be creative, to put his unique stamp on the episodes he shot. He had no idea what that meant for Bill Hines when he returned to *Catering to Dallas* after this personal leave. But hey, it wasn't his place to ask. He had a job to do and he intended to do it well.

Now that the whole cast and crew was together, instead of shooting right away, it would serve everyone well to have a meeting and talk about possibilities for the show and the progress he wanted to make while he was there.

He probably hadn't made the most favorable impression right out of the starting gate. But one of the problems he could see right off the bat was that the cast and crew sort of came and went as they pleased. That was hell on the budget. He was used to professionals adhering to a set schedule and giving their all to get the job done.

That wasn't too much to ask, especially since Aiden had voiced concerns over the show's future. If they couldn't streamline the budget and get the ratings up, the show might not be renewed for another season. It was easier to come in like a hard-ass and lighten up than the other way around.

He'd had his reservations about filling in as interim director on a reality television show. But the timing had been right. Negotiations for his latest movie had fallen through. So the plea from Aiden had come at the perfect time. Plus, he also liked the irony that reality television seemed like a first cousin of the horror genre.

When Hollywood had crowned him the king of horror for *Past Midnight*'s success, no one had been more astounded than Miles. He'd never intended to make a horror film, and he'd certainly never dreamed of making a career out of scaring the hell out of people. *Midnight* had been his final college project. It had started as a documentary he'd wanted to make, debunking a legend that had haunted his family for five generations. In the end, the project had driven a wedge between him and his father—because his father claimed he'd sold out his family. That so-called sell-out film had morphed into a career that continued to haunt him.

This sojourn in Texas would give him some time to think over his next move while he was helping out a friend. Maybe he could even start the healing process with his father. Regardless, he was going to see his mother and five siblings while he was in Celebration. He could only hope for the best with his father.

Miles joined Aiden by the camera, which was set up in the kitchen. "When do you want to get started?" Aiden asked.

"Now?" Miles said. "But let's start with a short meeting."

Aiden nodded and clapped his hands. The buzz on set stilled and the twenty-odd-member cast and crew looked at him. "Boys and girls, let's all gather 'round for a short production meeting before we get started with the next scenes."

As soon as everyone had assembled, Aiden began again.

"We're happy to have Miles Mercer with us while Bill is away on leave. While Bill is gone, the powers that be and I thought it might be a good idea to try some new approaches. As you know, *Catering to Dallas*'s first ratings aren't where we'd hoped they'd be. Since it's crucial that we have as little interruption to the shooting schedule as possible, Bill is completely on board with Miles's new vision for the show."

New vision? That might be a bit of a stretch at this point, Miles thought. He had some ideas, such as featuring Sydney, but he wouldn't necessarily classify what he'd come up with so far as a vision. After he'd accepted the gig, he'd done some boning up on reality TV, since it wasn't the type of program he usually watched. He'd studied some of the popular reality shows and reviewed the *Catering to Dallas* dailies and episodes that had already been produced. So he felt like he had a pretty good handle on the show, but he'd decided he needed to meet the cast before he could come up with a vision and determine the direction in which he'd lead them.

He had to hand it to the ladies. They all had class and style. But he also had to admit that he had a particular leaning toward the brunette with the stunning green eyes: Sydney James. In her role as the marketer and publicist for Celebrations, Inc., she was the most unassuming of the cast members. Yet, as he'd watched the footage that Aiden had sent him, she was the one who stood out. He was drawn to her, and always found himself wanting to see more of her on the screen.

"So without further ado, I will turn the floor over to Miles."

There was a smattering of applause, which caught him by surprise and pulled him out of his thoughts. Before, though, the old adage about faking it until you make it flitted through his head. "Thank you. I hope you'll still applaud once you hear my ideas." He laughed, and everyone chuckled along with him.

That was a good start.

"First, I want to apologize if we got off on the wrong foot this morning," he said. "I realize that I'm the new guy on the set, but I do like to run a pretty tight ship. All I ask is that you're prompt and professional and we will all get along just fine."

He didn't want to single out Sydney. So he didn't look at her. When they'd talked earlier, she'd been a good sport. Now, as he addressed the group, she wasn't making his request for punctuality personal like so many Hollywood starlets he'd worked with might have done. He detested people who caused drama for drama's sake. He got a completely different vibe from Sydney. It was refreshing.

"So what are we cooking up this afternoon?" he asked, changing the subject.

That time he did direct the question to Sydney, but A.J. answered.

"We have a wedding we're prepping for next month. It's a pretty big deal among Dallas society. The only daughter of cattle baron Rick Ronstead is getting married. Everything has to be first class all the way. So we have a lot of work to do to get ready for the event itself, in addition to shooting the footage for the show."

"The television show has added an interesting dimension to our work," Sydney chimed in. "Because even though we're filming for television, we still have to keep our clients' best interests at heart. Celebrations, Inc. is a catering company first. We're television personalities second. We have to keep in mind that this event is Tasha Ronstead's *wedding* and we must make sure that we do our part to make her day—and every event, for that matter—as special as it can be. We can't sacrifice our clients for the sake of good TV."

Miles found himself nodding and thinking that she was smart as well as beautiful, and judging by how protective she was of Celebrations, Inc.'s client base, she was obviously passionate about her work.

Who could argue with passion? Maybe he wouldn't argue, but he could test her a bit.

"That makes sense, but the challenge we face is balancing the need to create interesting TV and remain true to your clients. Surely they realize what they're signing up for when they agree to be part of the show?"

He held her gaze as he had when he'd glanced up and caught her looking at him across the room before they met. Only this time her eyes flashed in a way that kept his gaze from dropping down to her lips.

"Our clients do understand what they're getting

themselves into," she said. "Believe me, the show has added an entirely new element to my job. Not only do Pepper and I have to publicize the company and book our events, but it's our duty to make sure clients know precisely what they're getting themselves into when they agree to be on the show. We could never ruin a special event all in the name of making a scene that would be interesting for television."

"And have we filmed you in that capacity?" Miles asked. "In the client-relations arena?"

The question, which he'd delivered in all sincerity, seemed to take her by surprise. She crossed her arms over her chest.

"Well, no.... Not directly, I suppose," she said as if the possibility hadn't occurred to her before now. "I'm support staff, and I'm perfectly fine to remain in the background doing my job."

He loved her accent, but he refrained from asking her what part of the U.K. she was from. That seemed too personal—

"Do you know about the cookbook idea Sydney came up with?" asked Pepper, pulling Miles out of his reverie. "It's called *Single Ladies*. It's all about single-serving recipes. That might be a fun reason to bring her into the spotlight."

Sydney shot Pepper a scathing look and shook her head.

"Well, really, it's a collaborative effort," Sydney said. "A.J. and Caroline are reconfiguring the recipes and Pepper and I are writing them up and putting everything together in publishable form. It would be nice if we could feature the cookbook on the show, but it's not simply about me."

That wasn't something that would spike the ratings, but it was fresh and different. An idea he could run with for a start. "How close are you to publication?"

"We have publisher interest," Sydney offered. "But we're still developing new recipes—even if they don't make it into this edition. I foresee a *Single Ladies* empire."

"Is that so?" Miles asked.

"Absolutely," Sydney insisted. "A *Single Ladies* empire could only help the show. Don't you agree? It will speak to a segment of the population we're trying to attract as our audience."

"Absolutely," Miles said. "We could do something with that."

"As long as you don't solely attribute it to me," she warned. "This is a four-way partnership."

He nodded rather than pointing out that the current split of airtime wasn't at all equitable with her mostly in the background. Now wasn't the time to drive home that point. Not in front of everyone. He would use much more subtle means to accomplish that goal.

"But I do have an idea I'd like to share," she said. "If you will permit me to do so?"

"Of course," Miles answered. When she talked it gave him a valid excuse to stare at her unabashedly, at her wide-set green eyes and the way her full lips formed a perfect cupid's bow.

"Perhaps it would be a good idea if Celebrations, Inc. and *Catering to Dallas* could do something where we give back to the community. That's always a win-win situation. The community benefits and we get good press."

"Did you have something special in mind?"

"Actually, I do." Sydney looked at her friends. "The girls and I have already tossed around this idea. So Pepper, A.J., Caroline, feel free to jump in at any time."

"You're doing a great job," said A.J. "Run with it."

"We were talking about giving away wedding catering services to a bride and groom. Perhaps we could film the selection process—choose a handful of finalists and narrow it down to one lucky couple. Maybe we could even get the public involved by allowing them to vote on the winners."

"That sounds like a great idea," Miles said. It was a slight departure from what they'd been doing, but it still remained true to the feel of the show. Plus, anytime there was a contest, it always drummed up new viewers. "Good ideas, everyone. I'd love to hear more about it now, but we're already behind schedule. So we need to get back to work. But, Sydney, let's you and I schedule some time to iron out the details. Sound good?"

Miles certainly hadn't turned out to be the monster her friends had portrayed him to be earlier that day, Sydney thought as she drank the last sip of her wine.

Given that *Catering to Dallas*'s twenty-six member cast and crew had gathered at Murphy's Pub to welcome Miles to the team, it was proof that no one harbored resentment or other issues from the morning.

Since Sydney hadn't seen exactly what had transpired and liked him well enough to go out on a Monday night to toast his arrival on the show, the only conclusion she could come to was that this morning had probably just been a misunderstanding…possibly perpetuated by the not-so-minor detail that no one had known where to locate her in the midst of the director-change storm.

Looking back on it from this vantage point, it probably hadn't been the wisest move to leave the country without telling anyone where she was going.

Oh, well, what was done was done. There was no need to fret over it now. And there was no need to tell anyone about the job interview just yet. Not unless she made it to the next level of the process.

Time would tell.

In the meantime, there was a welcome party going on and she fully intended to enjoy it. Especially when Miles came back from the bar with a fresh beer and a glass of white wine, which he placed in front of Sydney. He planted himself in the seat beside her and took a long draw of the beer. When they'd first arrived a couple of hours ago, he'd been sitting at the opposite end of the table with Aiden and some of the other crew members. She'd been talking to the girls. Every once in a while she would glance up and catch him looking at her. The first couple of times she'd looked away. Then she'd decided to join him in his game, cocking a brow, raising her glass to him. If she hadn't known better she might have thought he was flirting with her.

And now he was bringing her wine.

"Thank you," she said.

He nodded and touched his beer bottle to her glass.

"Good to see that this is still a pretty happening place for a Monday night," he said, glancing around the bar. Sydney followed his gaze, trying to see Murphy's through his eyes and then remembering he grew up in Celebration. It was probably more familiar to him than it was to her.

"Did you come here a lot before you moved away?"

The corner of his mouth quirked up into a half smile. "Well, not as much as I would've liked to since I was underage."

Murphy's was one of Celebration's best-loved spots. It was a casual place where anyone could drop in for a drink or a respectable offering of pub food.

A long wooden bar, staffed by bartenders who had been there since the beginning of time and could mix any drink known to mankind, ran the length of one wall. People were dancing to songs from the sixties, seventies and eighties that drifted from the jukebox in the corner. A couple of pool tables occupied the left side of the room. They always seemed to be in use. Booths and tables filled in the rest of the room.

Sydney spied Aiden shooting pool with Caroline's husband, Drew, who was the editor-in-chief of the *Dallas Journal of Business and Development.* For a split second, she wondered if she should go over and see if Aiden was pitching Drew a story about Miles's arrival. Public relations and dealing with the media was her area of expertise, after all. However, she was off the clock and a little looser from the wine. Even though his arrival would make a good news story—Hometown Boy Who's Done Well Comes Back to Work on Locally

Filmed Show—Aiden could handle it…or it could wait until tomorrow.

She turned her eyes on Miles.

Maybe it was the combination of the wine and exhaustion, but she suddenly felt very relaxed sitting there. Miles had just sat down and she didn't want to be rude getting up to talk to the press, especially when the press in question was her good friend's husband. "Did you leave for college right after high school graduation?"

He shook his head. "I joined the army right after I left Celebration."

"You were in the service?" Sydney asked. The e-encyclopedia hadn't mentioned that.

He nodded as he took another long draw of his beer.

"How did you go from soldier to scary filmmaker?" The place was noisy and she leaned in a little closer to hear what he had to say.

"I've always loved film," he said. "I even shot when I was on active duty, but then I was injured."

She thought she'd noticed him walking with a subtle limp. "So, you're a war hero?"

"That's stretching it a bit," he said. "I wouldn't go that far."

He didn't strike her as the type to fake modesty. "What do you mean?"

Everyone else had either gotten up to dance or shoot pool or was engrossed in conversation within their own huddles. The music was so loud, they were sort of in their own little world. It was nice…and intimate.

"It's a long story," he said.

"I have all night."

"Do you?" he asked.

That was a loaded question, and there was something in the inflection of his voice that she could've taken all sorts of different ways if she'd wanted to.

Instead, she smiled at him and said, "Relatively speaking."

"I'll make a deal with you," he said. "You tell me where you were this weekend and I'll tell you about how I was injured."

As the jukebox switched to a mournful country tune, a guy singing something about wasted days and nights, those who were dancing moved close together and swayed to the rhythm. "Why do my whereabouts on my free time matter?"

"I'm just curious," he said. "But technically, you were MIA on my watch. Even if it was only a few hours." The corner of his mouth quirked up in an unexpected touché, and the raw sexual energy that danced between them made her want to reach out and touch him.

"If you don't want to talk about it, I respect that." His voice was low and husky and when she looked at him, she thought, *bedroom eyes*.

She had to look away, or risk getting caught in the magnetic net of this chemistry. Temptation plus wine equaled a whole slew of ways she could get in trouble. Not to mention, she hadn't even told the girls about her trip to St. Michel.

"So you consider Texas home?" she answered.

Miles shrugged. "I was born and raised here. I haven't been back in a long time."

"Do you still have family here?"

"I do. Most of them live here. The Mercers are a big, rowdy brood."

"Are you close?"

She watched him as he stared at his beer bottle, picking at the edges of the label. "My mom and I are close. She's really the glue that holds the family together. And my siblings and I stay in touch as much as we can. I've got three brothers and two sisters and some of them are married with kids. Everyone is just so darn busy these days. You know? It's hard for most people to get away—even if it's just for a long weekend. Maybe they should take lessons from you since you seem to be so good about juggling a career and flying off to parts unknown."

He had a mischievous glint in his brown eyes. For a moment, the way he was looking at her made her breath catch under her breastbone.

"Okay, it's obvious you're not going to let this go, are you?" she said. "So if you must know, I had a job interview. But please keep it between you and me. There's no sense in getting everyone all excited about it if I don't get the job."

She had no idea why she was confiding in him. She'd simply drawn in a breath and the words had spilled out of her mouth before she could contain them, but she'd already spilled the beans. So now she had to live with it.

"Your secret is safe with me," he said.

"You're not going to tell? Or even blackmail me?"

"Blackmail's a great idea," he teased. "Yes, I'm glad you brought it up because I can definitely use it to my advantage."

"You do realize there are laws that prevent that type of harassment?"

"Of course. I was thinking more along the lines of trying to find some way to entice you to stay."

She was leaning in again. Or maybe he was the one who'd moved closer. But there was definitely something going on here. Even though every fiber of good sense in her being told her fooling around with the boss wasn't a good idea, her libido was wanting no part of playing the good girl.

Chapter Three

Several cars were parked in the suburban cul-de-sac of Miles's parents' neighborhood. He stopped the car at the first break in the line of vehicles and parallel parked along the curb. He sat there looking at his childhood home for a moment before he killed the engine.

The last time Miles had come home, the visit had been a disaster.

He drummed his fingers on the dashboard, wondering if this was a mistake. Maybe he should've met them out somewhere, on neutral territory.

But no, he was doing this for his mom. For that reason, he reminded himself that this time things would be different. Even if he had to bite a hole in his tongue. Lightly, he closed his teeth around the tip of his tongue as if giving censure a practice drill.

His mom was the peacemaker of the family and deserved better than the scene that had unfolded between Miles and his father the last time Miles had come home for a visit. Five years ago.

He and his dad hadn't spoken since. Even if Miles couldn't go back and change what happened on that day, he could take the high road and move forward.

For his mother's sake.

He unlatched his seat belt and let himself out of the car. The sturdy brick, two-story Colonial, which was surrounded by trees, sat atop a small hill and seemed to be looking down on him as he made his way up the paver-lined driveway. It wasn't the most fashionable house, especially not compared to some of the homes in Hollywood he'd visited, but it was a family home, warm and inviting, well-kept with a lived-in patina. He had to hand it to his old man. The guy would make sure his yard was manicured if he had to crawl around on all fours to get it done.

Window boxes sported bright red geraniums. There were two white wicker rockers on the front porch that looked as if they'd recently received a fresh coat of paint. A closer look revealed that the seat cushions were fraying, but the paint made the chairs look nice and inviting, even if they weren't brand new. That was his mom's handiwork. So was the sunflower wreath on the front door. All these little touches made a person feel welcome and wanted.

If that didn't sum up the difference in his folks: his dad tended to the practical matters like the lawn, weeding and edging, while his mom added the nice touches that made this middle-class house a home.

When he'd talked to his mom to tell her he'd be back in town, she'd assured him his father would be heartbroken if Miles stayed away.

"Mom, Dad and I haven't spoken in five years. What makes you so sure he's so eager to see me now?"

"You just leave everything to me, honey. I'll deal with your father and he will welcome you as warmly as if nothing ever happened. Trust me."

That was another thing about his mom: when she got her mind wrapped around something—especially if it had to do with her family—nothing stood in her way. She was a woman of her word. So when she said, "Trust me," she left no alternative.

As he climbed the brick steps toward the red front door, a calico cat he didn't recognize sprinted past him, making him do a stutter step so he didn't step on it. The animal stopped under one of the rockers, eyeing him warily.

"Don't believe a word he told you about me," Miles murmured. "It takes two to box."

Actually, his father had never laid a hand on him in anger. His words had always been his most powerful weapon. It was his military background that made him that way. Miles Mercer III was an army man through and through. He did everything by the book—well, his own interpretation of the book—and expected everyone to conform and follow suit.

Few were brazen enough to dispute him, because

when you did, well…you paid the price. In Miles's case the price was exorbitant: excommunication.

For a moment, he stood there watching the cat watch him, realizing he wasn't sure if he should knock or walk in. This had been his home for the first eighteen years of his life. At twenty-nine, he'd still spent more time under this roof than anywhere else. But things were different now. As his father had so aptly pointed out the last time Miles had walked out this door—the last time they spoke—this was no longer his home.

He pulled back his hand and landed three sharp raps with his knuckles. In less than ten seconds the door swung open and his mother's squeal of delight pierced the air.

She threw her arms around him.

"Miles, my baby boy. I cannot believe you are finally home." She pulled away from him suddenly and held him at arm's length. "I just want to look at you for a minute. I cannot believe you are finally here."

Tears made her eyes sparkle.

"Hi, Mom," he said, unable to suppress a smile. "It's great to see you."

She looped her arm through his and walked inside. "Everyone! Everyone! Come here! Miles is home."

As if someone had opened up the flood gates, about twenty people crowded into the foyer, each of them talking at once and nudging each other out of the way to give Miles hugs, handshakes, high fives and slaps on the back.

His three brothers, Christopher, Grant and Ben, were there. His oldest sister, Patricia, her husband and their four kids were in the mix and over in the corner, he spied his baby sister, Lucy, hanging back from the rambunctious group, studying the display screen on her phone like kids these days tended to do.

She looked up and flashed him a shy smile and gave him a little wave. Miles gave her a salute and she laughed and rolled her eyes.

That's when he saw it. She wasn't such a little kid anymore. She had to be what—he quickly did the math in his head—she had to be fifteen years old by now. He'd sent her birthday presents every year, mostly cards with money tucked inside, but he was floored by how the years had stacked up and flown by.

He also noticed that his father was not among the greeting committee. For an instant a thought burned inside him that maybe the old man had skipped out on the occasion. Then Miles took a deep breath, swallowing the bile burning his throat and forced himself not to jump to conclusions. That's when he realized his mom was cooking something that smelled delicious. He breathed in again, this time letting go of the simmering anger and enjoying the familiar sights and scents of home.

As if reading his mind, his mom asked, "Are you hungry?"

"Starving," he said. "Whatever you're cooking smells like exactly what I'm hungry for."

"Okay, everyone take a step back," his mom ordered. "Give Miles some room to come inside the house."

The family obeyed, except for a little girl who looked

like a pre-teen, lingering in the foyer looking up at him expectantly.

"You're not Zoe, are you?" he asked. She beamed up at him, nodding her head.

"Naah, you can't be Zoe," Miles teased. "Zoe was just a tiny little girl the last time I saw her. You're a teenager." A slight exaggeration, but something told him saying that would make her smile.

"I *am* Zoe and I'm ten," she said. "Do you work in the movies?"

"I do."

"Do you know Justin Bieber? Has he ever been in one of your movies?" Her hazel eyes shone as bright as the sun.

"I hate to disappoint you, but Justin Bieber has never been in one of my movies. I did see him once at an awards show in California."

Her mouth formed a perfect O.

When she recovered, she asked, "If you ever put him in one of your movies, can I meet him?"

"You've got a deal," Miles said. "If he's ever in one of my movies, I will make sure your mom brings you out to California to meet him."

"My mom's your sister, right?" she asked as they made their way into the family room.

"That's right," he said.

"So you're my uncle, right?"

"Yep, and that makes you my niece."

"Cool!" she said and ran off to another part of the house, yelling to anyone who would listen that she was going to meet Justin Bieber someday soon.

As Miles made his way into the living area, he glanced in the open door of the office, which was located between the family room and kitchen. There he glimpsed his father at the desk concentrating hard over notes he was making on a yellow legal pad. Miles hesitated, wondering if he should go in and say hello, but mostly hoping his father would look up, see him standing there, and break this insidious wall of ice that had stood between them since they'd last exchanged words.

Before Miles could say anything, his brother Ben came up to him, clapping him on the back. "Hey, Mr. Hollywood, it's about time you came home. Come over here, I want to introduce you to my fiancée."

What? With one last glance at his father, who was still presumably caught up in his work, as if nothing were going on outside of the ordinary day-to-day grind, Miles followed his brother into the kitchen where a pretty blonde was talking to his mom and making a salad.

"You're getting married?" he asked.

"We are," Ben said. "Miles, this is Jeanie, my future wife."

The blonde beamed as she wiped her hands on a dish towel, held up her left hand to show off the modest diamond on her ring finger, and then enfolded Miles in a hug.

"Congratulations," Miles said, suddenly realizing that life in Celebration had indeed been speeding on without him. Not that he expected things to come to a screeching halt, but having been away for five years, the differences were more pronounced—children were growing up, his younger siblings were getting married and making lives of their own.

"When did this happen?" he asked.

"Two weeks ago," said Jeanie.

"Have you set a date?" Miles asked.

"Not yet," said Ben. "We wanted to talk to you to see when you thought you might be available. You're going to be my best man, right?"

"O-of course," Miles stammered. "You just tell me when and I'll be there."

One of the other nieces, Ivy, came and got Jeanie to turn one of the jump-rope handles in a tournament she and the other kids were having on the porch.

"Well, sweetie, I'm helping your grandma get dinner on the table," she said.

"Oh, no, you go on and play with the kids. I'll finish up here," Deena said.

Jeanie thanked Deena and flashed Miles an apologetic smile. "I'm going to play with them, but we will talk more about the wedding later, okay?"

"Of course," Miles said as his brother's *fiancée,* allowed the little girl to lead her away. *Fiancée.* The reality that his little brother was engaged blew him away. He couldn't quite get his mind wrapped around it.

"We just love Jeanie," his mom said. "We would love it if you would settle down, too. No pressure, though."

For some reason Sydney James's face flashed through Miles's mind—the way she looked last night in the dim light of Murphy's as she sipped her wine and spilled her secret about the job interview with that accent that made him more than just a little hot and restless. He intended to keep her secret, but he also intended to entice her to stay. She was exactly what *Catering to Dallas* needed and somehow he would convince her that she needed them just as much.

"Are you staying for game night, Uncle Miles?" asked his sister's oldest daughter, Sally. "We usually have game night on Saturday night, but it's a special occasion since you're here and Grandma said we could have game night tonight. Will you stay? *Pleeease?*"

"We'll see," Miles answered. "Sounds like fun."

Saturday night family game night was another long-standing tradition in the Mercer household. Miles was glad to see it still prevailed. Back in the day, his friends used to come over and hang out. Sometimes they'd stay over. His mom prided herself on providing the kids with a place where they were all comfortable. His dad had been on active duty back then, on assignment wherever the army sent him. He petitioned for assignments at Fort Hood—or as close as possible—and sometimes he got them. But when his dad had been sent to places far away, his mother had been adamant about maintaining a normal life for her kids, giving them a permanent home base. Looking back, it seemed like their father was away more than he'd been home. Miles wondered how a marriage could've survived under those circumstances. Then again, his parents were built for the long haul. That's just how his folks operated.

As various friends and relatives drifted in and out, hugging him, asking for the quick catch-up, Miles had a chance to take in his surroundings, marveling at how it all looked the same as when he was growing up, only now he saw it through a different lens.

The lower level of the house was an open floor plan with the kitchen, family room and a casual dining table contained in one area. The space that had once seemed so large looked a little smaller than he remembered it. The tile-covered countertops that he could vividly recall his mother being so excited about years ago looked a little worn and dingy now.

The same chalkboard from his childhood hung on the wall next to the refrigerator. The same linoleum that used to be a shade of off-white and was now leaning towards light gray, still covered the floor up to the point where the carpet in the family room began. It delineated the space where the kitchen ended and the family room started.

The same large, overstuffed sectional sofa sat atop the same Berber carpet that still looked brand new thanks to his mom's TLC and obsessive vacuuming.

He watched her as she stirred pots on the stove and checked something in the oven—it looked like meat loaf—and worried over something else in the refrigerator.

"Hey, Ma," he called. "Let me help you. What can I do?"

"Not a thing. You just talk to everyone and relax," she said. "Lucy can help me here in the kitchen. Lucy, I'm talking to you. Lucy!"

The girl looked up from her place on the corner of the couch where she'd been texting and pulled one ear bud out of her ear.

"What?" she snapped.

Miles saw his mother give her a look and the girl immediately straightened up. Miles was all too familiar with that look. It was a silent warning. If she didn't comply, the punishment would be worse than a court marshal. Deena Mercer's husband might have retired a sergeant first class, but she was the long-standing general of the Mercer army. She commanded respect and her family gave it to her.

"I think you know that the correct response is *yes, ma'am,*" Deena said.

"Yes, ma'am," Lucy answered. "I'm sorry. I didn't hear you." Miles could see the way the girl's hands were fisted in her lap, but her tone of voice was much softer now.

"Please put that cell phone down and come here. I need you to set the table in the dining room and the one here in the family room, and then set the picnic table out on the back porch for the kids. We need twenty place settings in all, please."

Lucy didn't smile, but she nodded and set about her duties, tucking the phone into the pocket of her jeans rather than setting it down as her mother had told her to do. Miles sensed something was up. His little sister had an edge that went beyond typical teenage angst and moodiness.

When the girl was out of the room, he asked his mom, "Is Lucy okay?"

His mother's face tightened and her mouth flattened into a grim line. She hefted the pot of boiling potatoes off the stove and dumped them into a large colander in the sink.

"It's been an interesting year," she said as she set the pot back on the stove and turned back to the sink to shake the remaining water out of the potatoes.

"Grab yourself a beer out of the fridge and I'll tell you about it," she said. "While you're over there would you hand me the cream, please?"

Miles handed the quart-size container to her and then opened his beer.

His brothers were occupied by a game of Mario Kart with the nieces. His older sister, Patricia, was following her toddler around making sure she didn't get into anything she wasn't supposed to. The others were out in the backyard, or grouped in various sets talking about one thing or another like big families did.

Miles pushed back the question of when his father might grace them with his presence. He hadn't materialized since Miles had seen him in the office, and after mulling over the expression his dad wore, he decided he'd be damned before he asked about him. Especially since he had these few moments alone with his mother, and he could tell she wanted to catch him up on what had been happening with Lucy.

"Thank you, hon," she said as she took the carton from him and brushed a lock of graying hair off her forehead. "Your little sister has been a bit of a handful this past year. She's had a hard time, but she's settling down now." Deena heaved a sigh and looked around, as if making sure no one was listening in on their conversation. Miles guessed she might've been looking for Lucy, who wasn't within earshot. He could see her through the sliding glass doors, standing next to the picnic table she was supposed to be setting, on her phone texting.

Pushing the envelope.

"About six months ago, your little sister snuck out in the middle of the night and went joyriding with that Phillips boy. She had no business being out with him at a decent hour much less in the middle of the night. He's *seventeen years old.*"

Deena gestured with the wooden spoon she'd been using to stir the butter and cream she was heating up on the stove. "The boy's parents woke up at about 2:30 in the morning, realized the car was missing and reported it stolen, before they realized their son had taken it. When the police found them, the boy was drunk. The police hauled both him and Lucy down to the station and made them call their parents, which was fine with your daddy and me because after that stunt, we'd reached our wits' end with that little girl."

Miles grimaced, thinking about what a nightmare that must have been for all involved. He'd pulled some pretty dumb stunts when he'd lived at home. Nothing as brazen as what Lucy had done—or at least he'd never been caught doing anything that stupid. Although his father would have an opinion or two when it came to the subject of Miles and stupidity. "So what happened?" Miles asked. "Was she okay?"

"Well, yes. She swore she hadn't been drinking. The police made her take a Breathalyzer, so I knew she was telling the truth. And of course the parents didn't press charges against their own son…although he did get into a heap of trouble over the underage drinking and driving. Lost his license, I think, and he'll probably be on restriction until he's thirty. I know we grounded Lucy for a very long time, even though the sheriff did a good job of scaring them both."

His mom looked tired. Under the kitchen's fluorescent lights he could see the creases etched into her face. There was a weariness about her that he'd never noticed before.

"After everything settled down and we had a chance to talk about it calmly, Lucy admitted she had been in way over her head with that boy that night. Apparently, he got a little *handsy*." Deena shook her head. "I think it scared her. Like it scared me to death." Deena was wringing her hands. "Just think of all the things that could've happened. I told her nice girls have no business out after midnight. That's why she has a curfew. Nothing good happens past midnight."

Miles winced at the irony of his mom's words. He half expected her to chuckle and say, "Sorry for the pun. I loved your movie, honey. Even if it was a little too scary for my taste."

Obviously, she hadn't realized what she'd said because she shuddered and gave her head a quick shake as if clearing it of the *what if* cobwebs.

"How are things now?" Miles asked instead of agreeing that nothing good had happened since *Past Midnight*. "Lucy seemed to hop-to when you asked her to set the table."

Deena's mouth flattened into a thin line. "Yeah, if

you don't count the preamble of sassiness. Well, she's not allowed to date or wear makeup until she turns sixteen. Unless we make a special dispensation like we're doing this weekend. She's going to a dance—with an age-appropriate boy, who does not drive. His parents are taking them. And really, she's been working hard at school and helping me around the house, basically keeping her nose clean and out of trouble. She's invited her daddy to speak at career day next month. That made him so happy. He's been working on his speech since the moment she asked him." His mother sighed again. "She made a mistake. I really want to believe she learned from it. You know what we've always said. Only new mistakes." Miles felt his father's presence before he heard him enter the room. Because when he turned around, Miles Mercer III was standing in the threshold between the family room and the office where he'd been holed up since Miles had arrived. He was regarding his son with a look that fell somewhere between neutral nonchalance and general irritation.

That's why Miles Mercer IV was shocked as hell when his father walked over, extended a hand and said, "It's been a long time."

Chapter Four

Deena Mercer had always maintained that Miles and his father were too much alike and that's why they clashed in such an explosive way. However, Miles couldn't stand the thought of being as stubborn and jaded as his old man. So, most of his life he had taken great pains to go the opposite direction.

That's why they clashed. Because he wanted to be nothing like his father. Then again, "clashing" hinted that two people were close enough to career off each other. Their problem resembled something closer to being drawn and quartered.

While last night's dinner had started out amicably enough with the handshake, his father had seized every opportunity to land a passive-aggressive verbal punch in Miles's direction.

For his mother's sake, Miles didn't take the bait. He ignored his dad's caustic remarks about Hollywood's fruits and nuts. When his father asked him when he was he going to settle down and get a *real job,* Miles had laughed it off. He'd also let it roll right off his back when his dad threw the barb about Miles's last two movies being flops.

"Can't win 'em all." Miles had shrugged it off, refusing to be goaded into a verbal altercation. He also decided there was no way in hell that he would admit to his father that he wasn't particularly fond of the idea of making horror films for the rest of his life. He was restless and discontent and looking for his next project—preferably something in another genre. That's why he was happy to have this breather working on *Catering to Dallas.*

"Guess not. Is that why you've come back here with your tail between your legs to work on that sissy cooking show?"

There had been a silence so chilling that his mother had finally piped up and said, "*Catering to Dallas* is a wonderful show. I don't care if you'd come home to work on a revival of the *Teletubbies,* honey. I'm just glad you're home. Dad—" Everyone had been calling him Dad for as far back as Miles could remember to avoid confusion, since they were both named Miles. "If you can't say something nice, just be quiet."

Then, without skipping a beat, she changed the subject, telling everyone about the annual block party that she and Dad were chairing this year.

As a career military man, Dad may have been a hard-ass, but his mother still ruled the roost. He had remained silent for the better part of the meal. After dessert of Deena's homemade chocolate layer cake, he'd excused himself to his office. He didn't say goodbye.

Miles Mercer III may not have offered the open-arm welcome that Miles IV had been hoping for, but at least he'd come out of his office and offered the initial handshake.

That's what Miles would focus on. Otherwise he might be tempted to come out swinging. He'd be in Celebration for at least a month. During that time he intended to make his father understand his reasons for writing and directing *Past Midnight* and make him understand he hadn't set out to disgrace the family name.

Today was a new day and he needed to put his family issues aside and focus on work. That wouldn't be difficult to do since first thing this morning, Miles was meeting with Sydney to go over her ideas for the Celebrations, Inc., wedding catering giveaway. The more he thought about it, the more he wanted to use it as a new story line on the show. Executive producer Lenny Norton had invited himself to the meeting, but that didn't dampen Miles's enthusiasm. Lenny had been out of town when Miles had arrived. They'd talked on the phone before Miles had come on board as the interim director, but today would be the first day the two would meet face-to-face. From what he understood, Lenny was a piece of work. The guy was a former cattle rancher who had sold his land and business and now had more money than knowledge of the television business. That was always the most dangerous kind of investor: one who didn't know a best boy from a boom operator, but wanted to be large and in charge. Apparently, that's what they were dealing with with Lenny.

Miles walked through the kitchen, where they were already setting up for that morning's taping, and into the hall where Sydney's office was located.

He rapped gently on the door.

"Come in," she called in her lilting accent. It made him smile.

He pushed open the door and found her sitting behind her desk. She wore a red silky-looking blouse that was a sexy contrast with her dark hair and green eyes. She looked better than Christmas and the Fourth of July all rolled into one crazy-gorgeous package.

She smiled back at him. "Good morning, Miles."

There was something about her accent that put him in such a good mood.

"Good morning," he returned, but his words were eclipsed by a crash that erupted out on the set. There was the sound of something breaking, glass shattering, someone yelling.

Maybe it was a set light?

They both grimaced.

"What was that?" Miles asked.

"I don't know," she said. "Whatever it was, it didn't sound good."

He took a step back out into the hallway and glanced down the hall into the kitchen. A big, beefy man he assumed was Lenny Norton stood in the middle of the kitchen gesticulating wildly, his loud voice carrying over the usual sounds of the crew readying the set for the first shoot of the day.

"Looks like a hurricane is blowing through the set. We're now short one tray of highball glasses."

"Lenny?" she asked.

Miles nodded and Sydney squeezed her eyes shut and sighed. "Come in, quickly, and shut the door. Maybe he'll get distracted and forget about us."

Miles did as she asked and settled himself in a chair across from her desk. They waited as if gauging whether or not Hurricane Lenny would blow their way.

"We might be safe," Miles said.

"Or it could be the eye of the storm," she answered. "It always gets eerily quiet when that happens and then *bam*."

They heard the boom of Lenny's voice again, but this time it sounded farther away.

"What is he saying?" Sydney asked.

"I don't know. I can't hear him."

Sydney came out from behind the desk and stood next to Miles as they both walked to the door and listened. They stood face-to-face and so close together that he could smell the scent of her fragrance, something floral and fresh, that made him want to lean in closer and inhale. They maintained eye contact as they waited and listened. Miles took a mental snapshot, wanting to learn her face by heart—the way her green eyes slanted down at the outer corners, the way her top lip was slightly fuller than the bottom one, the apple cheekbones that gave her such a patrician look.

Damn.

He sensed that she was the gorgeous, independent type who scared off the average Joe.

Miles had never been content to be average.

Hell, no.

The thought of the two of them being in cahoots, hiding out from Lenny, was kind of sexy. Even if it really wasn't such a conspiracy. No one enjoyed meeting with the guy, especially not first thing in the morning. However, since Lenny was the bankroll, he'd bought himself a say in all matters pertaining to *Catering to Dallas*.

Aiden, the cast and the crew had developed a tactic that was more of a sleight-of-hand diversion to distract Lenny from important matters. Still, sometimes when he caught wind of matters, as he had with this meeting, there was no getting around him.

"I wonder what he's going to break next?" Sydney said in a sexy, low voice.

"Do you want to get out of here?" The words were out before Miles could think better of it. "Maybe we could go downtown and get some coffee? Get out of this chaos?"

"I'd love to," she said without a second's hesitation.

She returned to her desk and grabbed her purse. As Miles opened the office door, they heard Lenny's thunderous voice booming down the hallway.

"Oh, no," she sighed.

"There's always the window," Miles joked.

"Don't tempt me." She made a sound of frustration low in her throat and put her purse back into the drawer. "But I'll definitely take a rain check on that coffee outside of the office."

Miles felt the thread of something catch between them. "Absolutely."

As she sat down at her desk, Lenny appeared in the open doorway. His considerable frame, clad in a plaid shirt, bolo tie and faded blue jeans, filled the space. A wide leather belt with a buckle that looked like a Longhorn steer head seemed to hold up his belly.

"Good morning, y'all," he said. "I've been looking all over for ya."

"We've been right here." Sydney shuffled papers on her desk, tidying up several stacks. She closed folders and returned pens to the mug she used as a holder, until everything was neat and in its place.

Eyeing her intently, Lenny took his seat in the chair next to Miles. "Are you this organized all the time, Missy?" he drawled.

"*Er*—my name is Sydney. I have to be organized or my job would be ten times more difficult," she answered.

Miles realized that until that very moment, he'd never loved the way the word *difficult* sounded. It was that accent of hers. It occurred to him that he could be quite happy listening to her read the dictionary for a couple of hours. They definitely needed to give her more on-camera time. She was an underutilized commodity. Although he doubted she'd appreciate being thought of in those terms.

"I know what your name is," Lenny said. "Missy is a term of endearment. So where are you from, Syd?"

She frowned and blinked, as if the question had taken

her by surprise, but as any PR person worth her salt would do, she recovered quickly. "England, originally."

"Did you grow up there?"

Her face shuttered and he could sense her backing away from the question. "No, I didn't. Is there some *Catering to Dallas* business you would care to discuss this morning, Mr. Norton?"

She folded her hands on her desk and smiled at him, the perfect PR professional.

"Lenny. Call me Lenny. And don't change the subject. Where did ya grow up?"

She raised a brow. "Why is that important?"

Lenny laughed. "Your accent is so upright and proper." He said the last three words with what Miles guessed was a butchered British accent.

"I moved around a lot as I was growing up." She looked down at her desk and shuffled more papers. "But I went to university at Oxford."

Oxford. That explained it. This woman was just as smart as she was beautiful, he thought as she pulled a folder from a desktop holder and opened it.

She glanced up over the top of it and snared Miles's gaze. A silent plea for help.

Miles cleared his throat. "So, Sydney, why don't you tell us your vision for this idea that you mentioned the other day? I think it sounds like a story line we should consider."

She shot him a silent thank-you with her eyes that seemed to go unnoticed by Lenny.

"That's exactly what I have right here." She lifted

two pieces of paper out of the folder and pushed them across the desk. "I've outlined it for you."

Lenny and Miles each took one and looked at what she'd written, but before either could say anything, she began going over her plan. "I see this as a way that *Catering to Dallas* can give back to the community. We give away a wedding reception to a bride who has done her own share of giving to the community. First, we will need to do a call for entries for local brides. We can do that locally, can't we? There would be no reason to broadcast it to the entire nation if we're just looking for women who are local."

Miles took a pen out of the holder on her desk and jotted down a few notes about issuing a call for brides. They would need to produce that spot ASAP. "Yes, we can do that. We will make arrangements with the local station to air it. Since it might even be considered a public service announcement, we can see if they'll run it several times during the day and evening. I admit that *public service* might be stretching it a bit, but there's no harm in checking into it."

Sydney nodded. "I'll follow up on that this afternoon. Really, we are offering a public service because we're looking to celebrate a local volunteer. We would be honoring and giving back to those who have already given to the community. To make the most of that, we could have a few finalists, maybe three, whom we would spotlight and highlight their service to the community. We post the finalists' profiles on our website, the public can have a couple of weeks to vote and we can film us going to the winner's house to inform her that she's won the reception. What do you think?"

"It's a great idea." Miles tried to steer the conversation before Lenny could jump in and spend his two cents.

Plus, since Sydney was excited about this story line Miles fully intended to make the most of it so that if she did get that job offer she'd mentioned, she might reconsider—or at least stay for the duration of his stint on the show.

"I think this is a good opportunity to show some contrast," Lenny said. "We could go with a 'rich bride, poor bride' theme." He made air quotes with his index and middle fingers.

Sydney frowned, but Lenny didn't give her time to speak. "That would be an angle that the community could appreciate," he said. "Give away a wedding reception to a needy bride and contrast it with the Ronstead wedding. *Rich Bride, Poor Bride* can be our own version of *Miss America Meets Honey Boo-Boo Child.* The public will eat that up faster than cheese grits on a breakfast buffet. What do you think?"

Sydney held up her hand and miraculously Lenny stopped talking.

"I think it's utterly horrendous," she said. "I could never exploit a family's financial misfortune, and I'd like to think that my business partners would back me on this. Besides, that misses the point entirely. This isn't about a needy bride as much as it is about a self-less woman."

She shot Miles a look and he read the *help me out*

message she was sending. They were getting good at reading each other's minds.

"Lenny, I have to agree with Sydney," he said. "Capitalizing on the misfortune of a bride and groom who can't afford a wedding just doesn't feel like *Catering to Dallas*'s style."

Lenny sat forward in his chair. His face had turned a light shade of pink. "Now, they would be aware of what they were signing up for. So it's no skin off anyone's nose."

"I think we have a difference of philosophy here," Sydney said. "It's one thing to honor a bride and groom for service to the community, but it's quite another to exploit the fact that they can't afford a wedding. I would like to stick to my original plan as outlined on this piece of paper. This way it's a win-win situation—a deserving couple gets the wedding of their dreams and Celebrations, Inc., looks good because we made it possible."

Lenny shifted in his seat. He moved the beefy leg, of which the ankle had been balanced on the equally beefy knee of the other leg, putting both feet on the floor. As he did this, he reared back and adjusted his longhorn buckle, then huffed as he got to his feet.

"I don't know about this," he said. "Personally, I think the *Rich Bride, Poor Bride* angle works best. It's more interesting. But let me think on it and talk to Aiden. Miles, you should sit in on that powwow, too."

"I'll be sure and do that," Miles said as Lenny walked out the door with a scowl plastered to his ruddy face.

Once the dust had settled, Miles and Sydney sat looking at each other again. Sydney shook her head.

"Well, that was a first-class disaster. *Rich Bride, Poor Bride*. That is so demeaning. How could he do that to a young couple?"

"Don't worry," Miles said. "It's not going to happen. I'll talk to Aiden."

"Thank you," she said.

Again, another thread seemed to connect them, linking them, pulling them slightly closer. Miles liked the feel.

"So you do realize that since this is your brainchild, we'll need to feature you on the show as you work to find your *Celebration's Bride?*"

"*Celebration's Bride?*" she asked and pursed her lips as if she were trying on the name. "I love that name. That's what we could call the contest. However, I don't want to be featured any more than I already am on the show. I have more than enough on-camera time, thank you very much."

She was more than a little sassy, but she was humble, and as genuine as the Hope Diamond. Two more things on an ever-growing list of qualities that made her so appealing.

"No, you don't have enough on-camera time," he said. "Right after Aiden asked me to come and fill in, I watched all of the *Catering to Dallas* episodes that have already aired and my eye was constantly drawn to you. Sydney, I definitely want to see more of you."

It was the strangest thing the way Miles's words made Sydney's stomach flutter and drop like she'd swallowed a swarm of winged creatures. They flew in formation in her belly.

She made a mental note to personally thank Aiden for bringing Miles into the *Catering to Dallas* family, but then she took the metaphorical black Sharpie in her mind and crossed the thought off the list with one bold, decisive stroke. Instead, she would thank Aiden for having the foresight and persuasion to get someone like Miles to fill in as *interim director*.

Because he wouldn't be here for long. Neither would she.

Yes, kudos for Aiden were absolutely in order. But what was she going to do with the butterflies in her stomach and the way her heart tended to switch to a staccato beat every time she caught Miles looking at her, which seemed to be more and more often each time she saw him?

The thing was, she liked it when his eyes were on her, despite the fact that he was her *boss*—even if it was for the short-term. He was too rooted in California—she wasn't exactly sure what that even meant, but the sentiment seemed right and distracted her from the fact that he was too sexy, too cocksure of himself and too young for her. Five years her junior to be exact. At their age, it shouldn't matter, but she was looking for all the reasons *why not* she could stack between them.

Her hands were in her lap and she could feel the moisture on them as she contemplated what he had just said. That he wanted to see *more* of her. Not to mention the suggestion that they ditch Lenny and get out of the office for coffee—and how she'd wanted to go.

Obviously, it wasn't just the thought of having the camera on her more than it already was that made her hot and bothered.

She rubbed her palms on her pants then fisted her hands so that her nails dug into her flesh. The sensation was a touchstone to help get her mind off the absurd possibility that there had been a double meaning in what Miles had said.

You know there was. It was as real as her rapid heartbeat.

It was the way he'd said it, despite the little voice inside of her head that warned that she was playing with fire, that *now* of all times was not the time to get distracted by physical attraction. Because she was already preoccupied with the possibility of moving back to St. Michel—and she'd told him her secret even before she'd told her best friends and co-workers....

Still, despite good sense and propriety, she heard herself saying to him, "You want to see more of me? Is that strictly professional...or personal?"

"Both," he said.

Chapter Five

The rest of that day and the next, the shoot was fueled by a certain private chemistry between Sydney and Miles. Or maybe it wasn't so private, as Sydney's girlfriends kept casting her curious glances, but it was certainly fun. She justified the flirting because it seemed to draw something out of her that she'd never before experienced on camera.

After defending her against Lenny and getting Aiden to go along with the *Celebration's Bride* contest title and story line rather than the ghastly *Rich Bride, Poor Bride* scheme, Miles seemed to also want his way so that the newest action on *Catering to Dallas* focused on Sydney planning the contest. She endured by going about her business and trying to pretend that the cameras weren't there. She thought of it as taking one for the team.

Sometimes it wasn't easy to completely forget about the cameras when a half dozen people piled into her small office with lights and reflectors, but just when she started feeling as if she'd had enough, she'd look up and see something in Miles's eyes that would entice her through to the next scene.

What a racket, she thought, now that she was at home, getting her house and herself ready for the weekly *Catering to Dallas* staff tasting that they held every Thursday night to test new recipes and select new menu items to offer their clients and feature on the show.

Really, the weekly staff tasting had become a social occasion as much as a work event. After all, they were a bunch of foodies who were working on a food-related reality television show. This gave them a chance to get together after hours. They cooked, ate and drank together in a more relaxed atmosphere than the one that found them constantly caught in the glare of the lights and cameras in the pressure cooker of a television show.

They rotated houses each week and this time it happened to be Sydney's turn to host. She was glad that for Miles's first time at their weekly gathering she would be on her turf.

It had been a long time since she'd felt this discombobulated over a guy. It felt good and fun and a little overwhelming all at the same time. At least she would be in her own house on her own territory. That helped quell the nerves that had knotted up her stomach. The fact that she was nervous over a guy she'd just met was another anomaly. How long had it been? Since Henri Lejardin back before she left St. Michel. She'd had it bad for him, but his heart had belonged to Margeaux Broussard. Ironically, it was because of Margeaux that she'd met Pepper, A.J. and Caroline. So even if the woman had stolen Henri's heart—well, *stolen* wasn't exactly the right word, *reclaimed* was more appropriate, because Henri's heart had never belonged to Sydney or any other woman except Margeaux.

However, Margeaux had been willing to share her friends with Sydney. These three women had become the closest thing to family Sydney had ever had.

How in the world was she going to tell them she was leaving— She stopped herself from worrying. The job in St. Michel wasn't hers yet. She'd fret over goodbyes if and when that time came.

Right now, she had to set out plates, napkins, silverware and wineglasses. And she only had a few minutes to change clothes and get everything done.

She went upstairs and changed into a blue halter-top sundress. It was July, the scorching days of summer. If she did move back to St. Michel, the one thing she wouldn't miss was the broiling Texas heat. While St. Michel was in the Mediterranean, thanks to the ocean breezes the heat wasn't as brutal as central Texas in the dead of summer. Here, it was enough to melt the asphalt off the roads that stretched through the rolling plains and grasslands.

Her time in Celebration had been well spent. She would take a lot of good memories with her, but, she reminded herself, it was time to go. Regret knotted in the pit of her stomach, but it conflicted with the overriding feeling that she couldn't alter her plans—especially plans centered around a dream job—for a man she'd just met, who might or might not be interested in anything beyond a fling.

As she filled a pitcher with ice and water, she thought about the questions Maya had asked her when she was in St. Michel for the interview: "What are you running from? What are you running to?"

Beyond the prospect of a good job, she couldn't answer Maya. She still couldn't. She would know it when she found it. In the meantime, that vague sense of restlessness goaded her along the path of discontent.

Miles's face popped into her head. So did Maya's words about *someone special* showing up for her in Texas. But Miles lived in California. There was nothing there for Sydney. He couldn't be *the one* Maya had spoken of.

Sydney laughed to herself. Here she was thinking about *the one* when she didn't even believe in all that soothsayer nonsense.

Her friends claimed that Maya had a special gift for bringing together soul mates. They even went as far as claiming it was Maya's enchanted chocolate that had led them to their husbands. Sydney was a realist, not a romantic. She was a good-enough friend to play along since her friends were all newly married and still living in the honeyed glow of newlywed bliss. However, she knew better than to kid herself. She didn't believe in soul mates, much less that someone could conjure a life mate with enchanted chocolate.

Besides, Maya hadn't given her any magical sweets—unless she'd spiked the drinking chocolate they'd shared as they talked. But Maya had eaten from that plate, too. So wouldn't the mojo do a number on the matchmaker, too? Unless she was immune?

The doorbell rang and pulled Sydney from her thoughts. She glanced at the clock on the microwave. Someone was ten minutes early.

Good, that just meant extra hands to help her finish getting everything ready. They weren't a formal, fussy group so not being completely ready for the gang wasn't that big of a deal.

As she made her way to the door, she vaguely hoped it might be Miles. As much as good sense warned her against it, she would've welcomed some time alone with him before everyone got there. Just some time to talk to him. Maybe to try and convince him that he really didn't need to put quite so much focus on her during the *Celebration's Bride* segments.

She opened the door and saw A.J. standing there with an exquisite bouquet of sunflowers and a box of candy.

Maya's chocolate? Really? The coincidence that she'd just been thinking about Maya's sweets and A.J. showing up on her doorstep with a box in hand gave her pause. Actually, it unleashed the darn belly butterflies that seemed to be her new pets these days, and made the hair on her arms prickle. Sydney crossed her arms in front of her and ran her hands down her forearms, smoothing down the silky hairs.

"I know I'm early," A.J. said. "But I come bearing gifts."

She thrust the offerings toward Sydney.

"Flowers and chocolate?" Sydney said dryly. "Have you come to court me?"

"You might say that," A.J. replied.

Sydney narrowed her eyes at her friend as she accepted the presents, handling the box of candy gingerly, as if it might infect her with the same love sickness that seemed to be epidemic among her friends.

Sydney was happy for them. *Really,* she was, she thought as she peeked inside the box of chocolates.

"Come in, A.J., please, before you melt or before the chocolates melt and you let all the cool air-conditioning outside. Where's Shane?"

"He's out of town. He sends his regrets and his love."

Shane Harrison was A.J.'s husband. They'd met two years ago when Shane had come to town on assignment with the army. It was love at first sight, and the two had happily settled into matrimonial bliss.

Since all of her previously single friends were now one half of a couple, the Thursday night tastings had expanded to include spouses and significant others.

"By the way, where exactly did you get a box of Maya's chocolates?" Sydney asked, as she and A.J. made their way into the kitchen. Truth be told, she wasn't sure she wanted to hear the answer.

A.J. looked at her like she had two heads. "At the corner convenience store."

It was Sydney's turn to give A.J. the hairy eyeball.

"Where do you think I got them?" A.J. said. "I ordered them. From Maya's Chocolate Shop. In St. Michel. That is the only place one can get Maya's chocolates."

"Of course," Sydney accepted, feeling that same strange sense of déjà vu she'd experienced when she'd met Miles for the first time. She chalked it up to coincidence, but she was hesitant to ask exactly why A.J. had bestowed such a gift upon her.

However, after about five minutes of obligatory small talk, A.J. got to the point.

"I came over early because I have something very important to ask you. A favor. It's a big deal. A *really* big deal."

A.J.'s serious expression caused a flicker of expression to cool Sydney's blood. "Sure, anything."

A.J.'s hand went to her belly, in what seemed to be a reflexive, protective gesture. As Sydney ran through a mental list of what might constitute *a really big deal,* dread knotted in her own belly. Was there something wrong with the baby?

"Is everything okay?" she asked.

A.J. sighed. "Actually, I have two favors to ask you. First, will you be my Lamaze partner? Shane's working a lot of nights and there's a chance he might be called away around the time the baby is due. I wanted to have a backup plan to make sure everything is in place."

Lamaze partner?

Oh.

Oh, *no.*

Sydney was so wrong for the job. Why in the world was A.J. asking *her?* It was like asking a little-league player to pinch-hit in the big leagues. She felt a little sick at the thought and had a sudden urge to leave the room, but she managed to control herself.

"Aje, don't get upset, but I have to ask, *why me?* Why not Caroline or Pepper? You've known them longer and they're…you know…a bit more kid friendly than I am."

"Caroline faints at the side of blood and Pepper has her hands full with Cody."

It was true. Despite Caroline's good business sense, she was squeamish. And Pepper had recently married Rob Macintyre, who had a disabled son from a previous marriage. While Pepper adored the boy, she did have a lot on her plate.

But did Caroline's aversion to blood make Sydney more qualified? That was debatable. Sydney had an aversion to *kids*. Well, that wasn't completely true. She had an aversion to the thought of having kids of her own.

She'd decided a long time ago that she wouldn't have children. Not after the horrendous childhood she'd experienced. Her mother had died, leaving Sydney a ward of the state. It wasn't her mother's fault, of course. One didn't have the luxury of planning when they departed. Death never came at a convenient time. But it was particularly difficult for a young child to be left alone in this world. She knew her mother would've done anything in her power to have seen her daughter through to adulthood, but all the love and wishes in the universe hadn't done a bit of good.

Life and death were so far beyond anyone's control that Sydney couldn't take a chance of leaving her own child in the same precarious position she'd been in. So the only good answer, the only safe solution, was to simply not have children.

Besides, selfishly, it left her free to pick up and go when it was time.

And it was time to go now, but how would she tell this to A.J.? It was too soon to bring it up. Perhaps if she didn't get the job, she could somehow find a way to help her friend.

In a sudden claustrophobic frenzy, a flash of heat enveloped Sydney. She went perfectly still. It was what she did when faced with a situation that made her feel caged. Lord knows she'd done a lot of running in her life. Taking the job in St. Michel wasn't running. Not really. It was moving on.

She inhaled a deep, calming breath and blew it out.

A.J. had obviously given this decision to ask her to be her Lamaze partner a lot of thought. Sydney's gaze strayed to the flowers and the candy. It obviously meant a lot to her if she would go so far as to bribe her.

Or perhaps it meant that deep down A.J. knew Sydney might say no.

Why would A.J. ask *her?*

Her of all people. The one who was least equipped to coach a friend on bringing a baby into the world.

"You do remember that I'm not particularly maternal, right?"

"I think you've never given yourself the chance to be maternal," A.J. countered. "When I look at you, what I see is someone who is smart, confident, organized. Someone who possesses a lot of common sense. Those are all the qualities needed for a good coach.

Plus, there's a chance that Shane won't be deployed. You might not even have to do it. So would you at least think about it? It would really give me peace of mind."

"Why not ask one of your sisters?" Sydney suggested.

A.J. leveled her with a stare. "Really? Syd, you've met my sisters. Which one would you pick to help you through something like that?"

She was right. Sydney wouldn't enlist any of A.J.'s sisters to help her out in a crucial time. They'd always been a bit preoccupied with their own lives. Sadly, A.J. had never been close to any of them. Still—

"I really don't know that I would be any better than the worst of them," Sydney said.

"That's not true and you know it," A.J. countered. "That's why I chose you."

To buy herself some time, Sydney turned around and walked to the cupboard. She took out a vase and filled it with water. The silence was deafening as she began trimming the flower stems so that they were the perfect height for the arrangement.

A.J. finally broke the silence. "Okay. So, you don't have to give me an answer now. Think about it for a while. But there's one more thing."

More? Sydney held her breath as she looked up into her friend's hopeful, smiling face.

Were those tears glistening in A.J.'s eyes?

Oh, no. Don't do that.

"Shane and I have talked about this at great length and we would be so happy if you'd agree to be the baby's godmother."

Sydney dropped the flower she'd been trimming and accidentally gouged herself with the shears.

"Oh!" she exclaimed, when what she really wanted to say was *bloody hell!*

"Did you cut yourself?" A.J. asked. "Are you okay?"

Sydney examined her finger and saw that it was just a small nick. She'd barely broken the skin. She turned on the faucet and held her finger under cold water—as much to cool down the new wave of claustrophobic heat that was closing in on her as to relieve her cut finger.

"See what a mess I am?" She couldn't look at A.J. "I can't even trim a flower stem responsibly. I'd be a terrible choice for a Lamaze coach, much less a...*god-mother.* A.J., did you not hear a thing I said?"

A.J. reached out and touched Sydney's arm. "You would be great. That's why we chose you."

Mercifully, the doorbell rang, giving Sydney a temporary out of this living nightmare.

A.J. gathered the flowers that still needed tending and said, "Here, let me finish this while you answer the door. But, Syd, think about it, okay? Please? I mean the godmother thing. We really think you'd be great. You're exactly the type of strong, independent woman we would want to raise our child if we couldn't."

Miles dried the last of the dinner plates and hung the damp towel on the oven door's handle.

The others had helped with the bulk of the cleanup, which was apparently standard practice with these Thursday night shindigs. Everyone was encouraged to bring original recipes to try out. Even though it was

July, tonight they were looking ahead to the holidays and trying recipes that would work for a Thanksgiving menu.

Tonight, there had been three different poultry main courses, four side dishes and three desserts. Miles's personal favorite had been the individual pumpkin mousses with brandied whipped cream.

Everyone had pitched in with the cooking. Those who weren't chefs, which basically meant everyone other than A.J. and Caroline, helped with the prep work and uncomplicated cooking. Afterward, everyone helped with the cleanup. It gave a whole new meaning to too many cooks in the kitchen, but there was a synergy and camaraderie about the evening. It felt like a big family—or at least a commune of like-minded people, if you didn't count Lenny, who had been remarkably subdued tonight.

As their coworkers had finished up and started to leave, Miles had purposely hung around, taking his time with the dish drying, looking for any excuse to stay.

"There you go, madam." He turned to Sydney, who had just put away the last of the silverware, and gestured to the clean kitchen with both arms outstretched.

"Thanks for staying and helping me finish up," Sydney said. "You didn't have to."

"I couldn't leave you to do the rest by yourself."

"Really, there wasn't that much left to do," she said. "But I'm glad you stayed."

Something hung in the air between them. Something so heavy it was almost visible.

"You're really great at this." Her voice was a little raspier than usual. "Can I hire you by the hour?"

"What exactly did you have in mind?" He cocked a brow and then smiled at her.

"Well, I was strictly talking about your cleaning services, but if you're suggesting something else, maybe we better finish this bottle of wine and talk about it."

"We probably should. We can't let it go to waste. And I certainly won't leave you to drink alone."

He watched her as she poured the rest of the bottle of cabernet into two wineglasses. He liked the easy banter between them, which seemed to happen so naturally. She was quick witted, and funny and smart. She had the most magnificent green eyes—the color of sea glass rimmed by a darker shade of jade that enticed him to stare a little longer than he should, trying to pinpoint their exact color.

When she turned to hand him one of the glasses, he set it down on the counter and took her hand and raised it to his lips.

From the moment they'd met, there had been an undeniable attraction between them that had sizzled into a certain kind of electricity. Since then, they'd been edging closer and closer to this moment.

As their lips brushed for the first time, unspoken feelings spilled over into a physical affirmation of how much he'd longed for her. He hadn't even realized how powerful this moment would be.

The kiss started tentatively. Slow and soft. Then it flared into a breathtaking explosion of ravenous greed, as if they were drawing their last breaths from each other.

Something, maybe it was the wine, made Miles feel a little dizzy. But the taste of her—hints of black currant from the cabernet and cloves from the dessert, and something intoxicating—righted the axis of his world, which, for a moment, had tipped and begun to spin out of control.

She had awakened something in him that had been sleeping, a hunger he didn't even know was possible.

There was a taste of promise and the forbidden. The two sensations collided and had him leaning into her, pulling her closer.

She slipped her arms around his neck and fisted her hands into his shirt collar.

He kissed her neck, and her head lolled to the side in rapturous abandon.

"This can't change anything at work," she whispered breathlessly. "In fact, I'm not sure this is such a good idea."

"What isn't good about it?" He traced her jawline with his finger and she shuddered.

"This," she said. Yet she didn't move away. In fact, she seemed to lean into him a bit.

"This?" He leaned in and kissed her again, softly and slowly.

"Yes, this." This time, she kissed him, then gently nipped at his bottom lip. "Isn't there a no-fraternizing rule at work?"

"Not that I'm aware of." He brushed her hair off her neck and kissed the tender spot behind her ear.

Her sharp intake of breath made his loins tighten. No-fraternizing rules be damned—if there was such a thing. There was something here that wouldn't be denied.

"I think we've already crossed that line," he said, "and even if we could turn back now, I don't want to."

But he did stop. He pulled away just a little bit and looked at her. "I don't want to force you into something you don't want to do, but I think whatever this is between us could be something good. So if you really don't want this, please tell me now and I'll walk away."

Chapter Six

On the first Friday of every month, Pepper, A.J., Caroline and Sydney always gathered for a girls' movie night. Usually, they used the opportunity to catch the latest blockbuster, but since it was A.J.'s night to choose the movie, and her husband was out of town, she'd opted to stay in and have the girls over for homemade Italian sodas, salted caramel popcorn and a movie on DVD.

"So, I've been dying to ask," said Pepper. "What's going on between you and our illustrious director?"

As if their radar had picked up on the utterance of Pepper's juicy question, Caroline and A.J. stopped talking and focused their full attention on Sydney, whose mind immediately flashed back to last night's kiss.

"What do you mean?" She put on her best innocent face, despite the way her brain was screaming, *We kissed! And it was heaven!*

In fact, when he'd asked if she wanted him to stop, that's how she'd answered his question. By giving him a long, lingering kiss. He'd kissed her back in a way that made her wish it could've lasted for days.

Even though she knew she had no business doing what she'd been doing, she couldn't resist him.

She didn't want to resist him, but that didn't mean the entire world needed to know. Especially because she was so confused about what to do. The girls would ask questions. They'd try to make the attraction into a great romance.

The logical part of her brain reminded her that now was the worst possible time to get romantically involved with a man she'd just met—that had become a constant inner monologue. But the other, foggier part of her head, reminded her that Miles's kiss had been the best damned kiss she'd had in a very long time. If the kiss was a benchmark, imagine what else he could do with that tongue.

Thank God good sense had overruled the promise of a very good time because that's all it could be— a short-term good time—and an hour or so after the kiss had begun, she'd ushered Miles out before things could get out of control. Before they really did reach the point of no return that Miles had talked about.

The thought left her breathless and she blinked it away as fast as she could. Sometimes it was as if Pepper had the uncanny ability to read minds, and her friend was looking at her as if that was exactly what she was doing now.

"You know what I mean." Pepper crossed her arms and eyed Sydney speculatively. "I've seen the way the two of you look at each other. So dish. *Now.*"

Sydney looked from one friend's face to the next, hoping she didn't resemble a deer caught in headlights. However, they definitely looked like hunters intent on bagging their prey.

"He's...*nice*," she finally admitted.

Pepper let loose a rather unladylike *whoot* and fist pumped the air. "I *knew* it!"

Pepper, their resident debutante and always the picture of decorum, never acted like this.

"Why are you making such a big deal out of it?" Sydney asked. "All I said was that he's *nice,* and it sounds like you're trying to pair us up. Hold up there, cupid."

"Then why did he just text you and ask when he could see you again?" Pepper held out a cell phone. Upon closer inspection, Sydney realized it was her own phone.

"What are you doing with that?" she demanded. "Give it to me."

Pepper complied. Sydney punched a few buttons, bringing the phone to life. Sure enough, there was a text from Miles.

Six simple words: when can I see you again?

And the cat was out of the bag. She felt her cheeks burn.

"Why are you reading my texts?" Sydney insisted.

"Your phone was on the coffee table," Pepper said.

"The text came up while you were in the kitchen. I wasn't trying to snoop. It just sort of popped up."

Sydney groaned.

"Why are you hiding this?" Caroline asked.

"There's nothing to hide." Sydney hoped her face was more of a stonewall than her wavering voice. She felt utterly and completely unconvincing.

"Syd, he wants to see you. *Again,*" said A.J. "Why are you fighting this? And just as important, why are you leaving us out? We need to love vicariously through you. You're our only single friend."

"Love vicariously?" Sydney scoffed. "Don't be ridiculous."

Her girlfriends might talk a good game when it was just the four of them, but A.J., Caroline and Pepper were all faithfully settled down.

Despite the fast girl talk about vicarious romance, all three of her friends were very happily married. They couldn't seem to understand why Sydney wasn't clamoring to get to the altar, too.

Sydney was elated for them and their happiness, but she didn't need to be paired up.

Aah, wait a minute. She had the sinking feeling that because of that text and Pepper's eagle eye, this girls' movie night might turn into a love intervention instead.

She did the math: Miles was an attractive, single man (even if he was a little young for her taste) and she was a single woman. It was a phenomenon that stretched all the way back to Jane Austen's days: the universal truth about single men in possession of good fortunes being in want of wives.

She had no idea of Miles's financial position, but she knew that she wasn't about to be roped or coerced or cowed into a relationship just because she was the only one of them that was still single.

Suddenly, she was feeling as if she'd become their project.

Maintaining long-term relationships with the opposite sex had never been Sydney's forte. Why on earth would she limit herself to one sweet in the man-candy store?

What fun would *that* be?

The man-candy store phrase that used to be her mantra rang dry and hollow. Still, just because she and Miles were single didn't mean they would be good for each other. She tried to convince herself that she wasn't interested in pairing up with anyone right now. Even though she knew in her heart of hearts that wasn't completely true.

She'd love to meet Mr. Right. She just wasn't sure he existed...or if Miles was interested in anything beyond the short-term.

But what was wrong with a fling...with a hot, younger man?

Really? No. Stop it.

Was this some sort of subconscious pattern? Most of the men she'd been interested in had been emotionally unavailable. And sure, there had been others, too, but certainly no one she'd ever wanted to commit to.

They'd simply had a good time while it lasted and went their separate ways.

Sydney remembered the feel of Miles's lips on hers. Just because she might be leaving soon didn't mean she had to take a vow of chastity. Really.

The thought set Sydney's stomach aflutter.

So her friends were all married and she was the only single lady on the set. This was definitely a glass-half-empty-or-half-full situation.

Half empty meant that in preparation for leaving, she would cut herself off from a romance, even if it was just a fling.

Half full meant she would have the fling and not overthink things.

Perhaps she needed to adjust her optimism glasses. She clicked the phone off and squared her shoulders.

"You wouldn't think less of me if I started seeing our boss?"

All three of her friends started talking at once, and while she couldn't make out exactly what they were saying, the general tone was happy and excited. It definitely sounded as if they were in favor of the possibility.

Sydney put her hands over her ears, the universal sign for quiet, and they piped down.

"Will you please text him back and tell him you want to see him ASAP?" said A.J.

"No, don't say that," said Caroline. "He'll ask to see you tonight, and we're certainly not going to give you up. This is our night with you. In fact, something must've been in the air because A.J. picked the DVD *Past Midnight,* because you've never seen it."

Sydney grimaced. "There's a reason I haven't seen it. I don't want to. I don't do scary, remember?"

"Well, darlin'," said Pepper, "You're going to have to buck up on this one. The first rule of landing a man is to know as much about him as possible. And your mission, should you choose to accept it, is to get a big taste of Mr. Mercer and share every delicious detail with us. So, this is the perfect place to start, right after you text him back and make plans for tomorrow."

Past Midnight was possibly one of the scariest movies Sydney had ever seen. Even if she hadn't seen many, she couldn't imagine anything much worse.

It manifested the kinds of uncomfortable feelings that haunted you long after the movie ended. It made you afraid to be alone in your own house. This was the reason Sydney didn't watch scary movies. She liked feeling safe and sound in her own space. Even though she wasn't a hopeless romantic, she'd take a happily-ever-after over a creep fest any day.

What made *Past Midnight* worse was that Miles had based it on a true story that had unfolded not too far from Sydney's own safe, secure sanctuary of a house. The basis of the plot was that Miles's great-great-grandfather had been accused of murder but ultimately acquitted. After the family had fallen on hard times, he'd sold off his land, the Whispering Willow Ranch, and the new owners kept discovering dead bodies on the land. Just five years ago, another body had turned up. The corpse was believed to have been a victim of the Whispering Willow Ranch murderer. The legend, which Miles explored in the movie, said that the ghost of the first person killed, a woman who was believed to be Miles's great-great-grandmother, kept dredging up the bodies. Even in the twenty-first century.

A quiver of anxiety shimmered in Sydney.

Bloody hell, who knew when or *where* the next skeleton would surface? Maybe when someone was out planting in their garden or when a golfer hit a ball off the green into the rough?

Sydney hugged herself, taking a few calming yoga breaths, trying to quell her rapidly growing unease. It was working until something tripped the motion detector on the backyard floodlights. She let out a little yelp and nearly jumped out of her skin.

"Curse you, Miles Mercer," she grumbled as she turned off the living room light so that she could see better outside. She wouldn't allow herself to think that the other reason she was standing in the dark was in case a person—alive or dead—had tripped it, they wouldn't be able to see her as easily. She did her best to stay away from the back window while still trying to see what on earth might have tripped the light.

"It was probably an animal of some sort," she said aloud. "An opossum or raccoon. Or an armadillo."

Did armadillos come out at night?

Her fright soon turned to irritation.

She was terrified because of a stupid movie. A stupid movie, based on a true story. Maybe she should've taken A.J. up on the offer to stay the night at her house. Sydney had said thanks but no thanks because A) she liked to sleep in her own bed, and B) she was afraid

A.J. might start pressuring her about the Lamaze class and the godparent situation.

A.J. had been good and not mentioned it again at the tasting or tonight at the girls' movie night. Sydney wondered if A.J. was being polite and giving Sydney her space to think it over or if she'd been maybe a little hesitant to bring it up in front of the other girls.

Would they get jealous? If so, then the one with the jealous streak would definitely be the best coach and godparent candidate. In retrospect, Sydney was sorry she hadn't tested this theory herself and brought it up tonight to see how the others would react.

The sensor light switched off, making Sydney jump again. She went to the windows and pulled the drapes. But that didn't make her feel much better or protected.

Another wave of ire flashed through her. She went to her purse and dug out her cell phone. The time display glowed 12:52.

She pressed a button and clicked over to her texts. Miles's texts flashed onto the screen.

Miles: When can I see you again?

Sydney: Tomorrow?

Miles: Why not tonight?

Sydney: I'm busy

Miles: Date?

She'd thought about texting back some glib answer or a :)—something vague to make him wonder. She finally decided that no answer might be the best answer.

Through the sides of the curtain, she saw that the sensor light had tripped again. A shiver racked her whole body.

The next thing she knew, she was ringing Miles's cell phone. She was sure she'd get his voice mail. At this hour didn't everyone turn off their ringer?

She was composing a terse but humorous message to the tune of how since she couldn't sleep after watching his horror movie, she thought she'd return the love and wake him up so he could keep her company.

She could be this "clever" speaking to voicemail.

"Hello?"

Oh, dear God, he picked up.

Her first impulse was to hang up.

But then he said, "Sydney?"

She squeezed her eyes closed tightly.

"Yes?" Her voice was stuck somewhere in the back of her closing throat.

"Everything okay?"

What were those terse yet humorous words she'd been crafting? She'd already swallowed them. They were nowhere to be found.

"Yes," was all she could manage, but then she decided to take another tactic. "I'm sorry to bother you, but I was thinking, we're way behind on choosing the *Celebration's Bride* finalists. We need to meet about that first thing on Monday morning."

She felt herself cringe in the ensuing silence.

"It's nearly one o'clock in the morning." His voice was flat. "You're calling me about work?"

Silence deader than the bodies that had turned up on the Whispering Willow Ranch stretched between them.

"No. Not exactly."

He chuckled, low and sexy and Sydney wasn't sure whether the sound soothed or irritated her. Was it possible for it to affect her both ways?

He could be the most infuriating man who had the most peculiar effect on her.

"Then, if you're not calling about work, it must be personal. What can I do for you, Sydney?"

The insinuation in his voice was clear. But she loved the way her name sounded as it crossed his lips. She closed her eyes against the heat that blossomed in private parts of her body that hadn't come alive in a very long time.

"Do you want me to come over?" he offered.

This was absurd. Of course, that's what he'd think she wanted. A *Past Midnight* booty call.

The reality of it was quite embarrassing.

"I'm sorry for bothering you Miles," she said. "I shouldn't have called so late."

"On the contrary." His voice had lost its teasing edge and sounded…sincere. "At least now I know whatever was keeping you busy tonight is over and whoever you were with isn't claiming you for the entire night."

Sydney drew in a quick breath. Why did it make her happy to know that the thought of her being *busy* tonight had bothered him a little?

"Would it have mattered if whoever I was with tonight *had* kept me all night? Because I considered staying the night."

There was more silence on the line. "I suppose it would depend on what kind of slumber party it was."

"I don't know what kind of party you would've called it," she said. "But I contemplated staying because I was too frightened to go home. And it's all your fault."

He chuckled. "*My* fault? I'm not the boogeyman. What did I do to frighten you?"

She walked to the refrigerator and drew water for the kettle to make herself a cup of herbal tea.

"It's that movie of yours," she confessed. "I'd never seen it until tonight. It scared the bejabbers out of me."

"I've always wondered," he said, "what exactly is a bejabber?"

"I don't know because I don't have any left," Sydney said. "They were all scared away."

"And it was my fault."

The automatic floodlight in the back clicked off.

"Yes."

"Well, then you must allow me to make it up to you."

"How exactly do you propose to do that?"

"My offer still stands to come over and…protect you."

"Somehow, I think that might be more dangerous than if I stayed here by myself."

The light in the backyard was off. Whatever had tripped it was gone. Or maybe the wind had settled down. She was breathing easier now.

"Then how about brunch tomorrow?"

Sydney caught herself smiling so broadly that her face hurt.

"That sounds lovely," she said. "What time should I be ready?"

Chapter Seven

The next morning, Miles picked up Sydney at eleven o'clock. She looked gorgeous in her yellow sundress that showed off her long, tanned legs. As he walked her to the car, he had to fist his hands at his sides to keep from touching her to see if her skin really was as soft and smooth as it looked.

Soon, they were sitting at an intimate table for two at Bistro St. Germain, chatting over orders of cedar-plank grilled salmon, salad niçoise and tall glasses of sweet tea. Minutes stretched into hours.

The conversation flowed so easily and naturally between them that they were soon confiding details of their lives that they'd never shared with anyone.

He'd known her less than a week. That was the thing about this woman. She wasn't just beautiful, she was smart and funny and so easy to talk to. It only seemed natural that they'd confide in each other.

"So you're saying that downtown Celebration remains almost completely unchanged from when you were growing up?" Sydney asked.

"It's like a step back in time," Miles said. "Like I never left."

"That's crazy," she said. "But it sort of reminds me of my past, too. It's like a little European shopping village with all its sidewalk cafés and connected storefronts. I love all the flowers in the window boxes and the awnings that stretch out over the sidewalks. They remind me of protective hands shielding the customers from the summer sun. Okay, that was a little corny, but it's true."

They both laughed. It wasn't corny. It was poetic and honest.

"I guess it just looks like home to me." Miles pushed up the sleeves of his blue oxford cloth shirt as he tried to ignore the emotional tug-of-war taking place in his heart. On one hand, it was good to be home; on the other, he and his father had a lot of baggage to sort out before he could truly feel at home.

To make matters worse, his little sister, Lucy, had called him asking him to speak at her school's career day. He knew she'd already invited their father. She'd hedged when he'd asked her if she could bring two guests. Then she'd gone on about how her friends would find Miles's job much more interesting than their father's.

"I shouldn't have invited him anyway," she'd said. "He'll just embarrass me."

Their mother had said several times how happy their father had been when Lucy had invited him as her guest. There was no way Miles was going to add insult to injury by usurping the career-day spot.

If Lucy could bring two guests, he'd do it. If not, maybe next year.

But today he was here with Sydney and that was all that mattered.

"That's not a very happy homecoming face," she said.

Before Miles realized what he was doing, he was telling her about his big, crazy family and how the majority of his clan thought his success was the coolest thing that had happened to the Mercers in ages.

However, ultimately, the movie *Past Midnight* had opened a canyon-size estrangement between his father and him. The long-standing rift, which they'd never discussed, still weighed him down like a metaphorical ball and chain.

"Have you seen him since you've been back?" Sydney asked as she sipped her water.

Miles nodded and ran his finger through the condensation that had collected on his water glass.

"That's a good start, isn't it?" she asked.

He shrugged as he weighed his words. "Hard to say. He was cordial, but his same old passive-aggressive tendencies surfaced before the night was over. Hey, how about we order some dessert?"

They decided to share the Bananas Foster. It crossed Miles's mind that he would sample every menu item Bistro St. Germain had to offer if it meant prolonging the day with her. Yet, even though it was good to be able to open up to her so easily, he didn't want to scare her off by dumping too much family drama on their first date.

After they ordered, she said, "So what does your mother think about this disagreement? Does she take sides?"

Miles laughed. "You obviously don't know my mother. She's equal parts Paula Deen and the Little General. Even though my dad is retired military, the family is my mom's army. She runs it accordingly. There is no way she would let a difference between my father and me interfere with the family dynamics. But you don't want to hear about this, do you?"

"Yes. I'm interested. Since I didn't have a big family growing up, I love hearing stories of other people's family dynamics. How does your father feel about your mother having the upper hand at home?"

"That's a good question." He pondered it for a bit. "I guess he doesn't mind. Really, it was necessary since he was away so much. My parents have this incredible relationship. They've been married for nearly forty years. Despite my dad's issues with me, he and my mom just seem to get it right. Even if they don't always agree, they love each other and they focus on what's important. As a couple, they have always been my inspiration. A reminder that true love really does exist. I need that sometimes living in L.A. Sometimes things seem so disposable out there. Especially relationships."

He could hear himself talking, but he couldn't believe he was saying these things to her, especially because she was looking a bit dubious.

"It's true," he said. "In a world of facades and make believe, my parents are my touchstone. Don't you believe in love?"

A pensive shadow darkened the shimmer of her green eyes. "I've never seen or experienced it."

"What about your friends? They're all married. You don't believe what they have is true love?"

She gave a quick, one-shoulder shrug. "I hope so. But they've each been married less than two years. Not that I'm saying they're not going to last. They just don't have the forty-year track record that your parents have. They're like the unicorn couple."

The label caught him by surprise and nearly made him choke on the sip of tea he'd just taken. "The unicorn couple? I don't understand. Is this a cartoon I'm not familiar with?"

"No, unicorns are mythological creatures. You hear about them, but has anyone *really* seen them? I equate true love with unicorns. Lots of talk about it, but who knows if it really exists?"

The server brought their dessert and they settled into enjoying it as the different topics they'd discussed ebbed and flowed.

Hmm, he thought, as he took a bite. He'd never talked about the validity of true love on a first date. Actually, he'd never talked about true love in any of his relationships.

He watched her as she lifted the spoon up to her lips and sampled the sweet. He had the sudden urge to lean in and see if her lips tasted even better than the creamy coolness of the vanilla ice cream and the simple sweetness of the warm caramel and bananas.

He'd wager that they would.

Then again, today, all his senses seemed to be heightened.

"How long have you been away from Celebration?" she asked, her spoon poised in midair in front of her mouth.

"Since I was eighteen," he said.

"Do you visit often?" she asked.

"I've only been back once, believe it or not. Once I left, and after the debacle with my father, I was basically gone."

"College?"

Miles leaned back and stretched, feeling strangely content in the midst of the good company, despite the fact that she was asking some pretty personal questions. Normally, it would set him on edge, but not today.

"Not immediately," he said. "Like I said, my dad is retired military. He wanted me to follow in his footsteps and join the service. I did. Not so much for the footsteps thing. I mean, serving my country was important to me, but it was also the only way I would be able to go to college without getting into debt over my head."

"What branch of the service?" she asked.

"Army."

"How long did you serve?"

"Four years. Then I got hurt and was discharged and then I went to college."

"Did you know A.J.'s husband, Shane, is in the army?

He's made a career out of it. In fact, he was supposed to retire right after he and A.J. got married, but the army keeps finding things for him to do."

"No, I didn't know that he's an army man. He wasn't at the tasting on Thursday night, was he?"

"No, he's been out of town for a few days."

She sighed and made a face.

"What's wrong?" he asked.

She waved away his question. "It's nothing."

"I explained my not-so-happy homecoming face," he said. "Since I've basically been an open book for the past," he pulled up his sleeve and glanced at his watch, "three and a half hours, it's your turn to share."

"Oh, my gosh, have we been here that long?" she asked. "I don't want to monopolize your entire Saturday."

"Why not?" he asked. "I was hoping to monopolize yours. And don't think that I didn't notice how you're trying to change the subject on me."

He smiled at her, loving the way that she looked down but then back up at him through long, dark lashes.

She nibbled at her bottom lip, and he could see the wheels turning in her mind, the virtual weighing of whether or not she'd share.

"So hypothetically speaking, of course," she finally said.

"Yes, hypothetically, of course."

This time her mouth curved in a smile of surrender.

"What would you do," she said, "if a friend asked you to do something you didn't think you could do?"

"Is this a peer-pressure situation?"

"*What?* No, now be serious. You asked me to tell you, but I'm not going to if you're going to make a joke out of it."

He sobered. "I'm sorry. I was trying to be funny, but it obviously didn't translate."

"Yes, don't quit your day job to pursue comedy."

He nodded. "Thanks for the tip. I'll take that to heart. Who's trying to make you do something you don't want to do?"

She grimaced. "It's not that I *don't want to*. It's more that I'm afraid I'm not capable."

Recognizing that this truly did seem to be causing her pain, he turned toward her and gave her his full and serious attention.

"Could you tell me more about the situation?" he said. "I'm having a hard time believing that there's much that you're not capable of."

She stared at the bowl of dessert that was slowly melting and set down her spoon. "A.J. asked me to be her Lamaze coach and her baby's godmother."

"Isn't her husband supposed to be the Lamaze coach?" Miles asked. "I've heard that's how dads feel they're a part of the birthing situation."

"I see you know your Lamaze. Is there something else you're not telling me?"

The way her eyes sparkled made his heart clench.

"Yes, that's why I asked you to have lunch today," he said. "I needed to tell you, I'm pregnant and you're the mother."

Sydney held up her free hand. "Haha. Sorry, honey, you'll have to go that one alone. I'm not mother material. That's exactly the point I've been trying to make A.J. understand and she won't hear it. I could probably handle the birth coaching part if she couldn't find anyone else. Really, I'd just be filling in on the slim chance that her husband is deployed before she goes into labor. But the godmother part. That's for life. I just…don't think I can."

"So, you're serious about not wanting to have kids?" he asked. It shouldn't matter, but somehow it did. In a flash, he saw her holding Miles Mercer V. Visions of the three of them as the perfect, happy family. But that was ridiculous and he shook the thought away.

"No." The single word she uttered was so quiet, it was barely perceptible. There was a sadness in those two letters and it seemed to suggest her outlook on her entire future.

Miles would've let it go—he knew he *should* let it go—but Sydney didn't seem happy about this definitive verdict.

"I know this is none of my business, but is that because you can't have children or you don't want them?"

"The latter," she said. She didn't seem as if she minded him asking. That's how this entire day had gone. Each of them asking tough questions and the other openly offering candid answers. "As far as I know I'm not infertile. Not that I'll ever put it to the test. But that's beside the point. I wouldn't make a good mother. Therefore, I wouldn't make a good godmother to A.J.'s baby. But she won't hear of it."

He wasn't quite sure what to say, how to advise her.

"Does she know about your job interview?"

Sydney snapped her head to look at him, her eyes wide. "No, I haven't told her. I'm sure I probably don't have to say this to you, because I trust you, but please don't mention anything about it to *anyone*. The verdict on whether I get the second interview will come in due time, I'm sure, and if I don't get a callback, there's no sense in getting everyone in an uproar. Especially with this latest Lamaze/godmother twist. That adds an entirely new wrinkle to the matter."

"Hypothetically speaking," he said. "Let's say that you don't get the job."

She shot him a look. This time he was the one who held up his hands in self-defense. "I know, it's unheard of, but let's just say for the sake of argument, the king of St. Michel wouldn't recognize a jewel if it fell out of his crown and he passes you over for some baboon—"

"The queen," she said.

"Excuse me?"

"It's the queen of St. Michel who holds the power. She's the one with royal blood. She actually married her security guard, which I find very romantic. But she's the one with the power and the jewels and I'm fairly certain that she can, in fact, discern the difference between a jewel and a baboon. She's somewhat of a friend. Or should I say, a strong acquaintance."

Okay, so smart, beautiful, funny and well connected. This woman was the entire package.

"I said we were speaking hypothetically. I didn't mean to insult your friend-acquaintance. But what I was getting at was, if by some fluke you don't get the job, will you agree to be her Lamaze coach?"

Sydney pursed her lips, and looked as if she were giving the possibility its due diligence.

"I suppose I could agree to that, but just the coaching gig. Not the godmother part. Because her baby deserves better than me and what I can offer…" She trailed off and her gaze became far away.

He reached across the table and took her hand. "I don't understand why you would say that," he said. "You have a lot to offer."

She inhaled a deep breath, but she didn't let go of his hand. "I've not had much experience with *family*."

She looked so sad.

"What do you mean?" She'd mentioned she didn't have a big family growing up. Was she estranged from her folks? Really, he couldn't imagine much worse than the bad blood that had pulsed between him and his father these last five years. However, he hadn't let it rip away the rest of the family.

"I grew up in foster homes. I never knew my father. My mother never spoke of him, and then she died when I was seven. Believe me, that's no life for a child. That's the reason I've decided not to have children."

Miles sat back and stretched his arm along the banquette. Sydney's emotional revelation suddenly had him appreciating the fact that his own family was intact. Because of that, maybe relations with his father weren't beyond repair.

He cleared his throat, knowing she wasn't going to like what he had to say, but he owed it to her to at least throw it into the mix.

"But if you agreed to be A.J.'s baby's godmother,

you would be saving the child from being in the terrible situation you were in, should—God forbid—something happen to A.J. and her husband."

Miles had a point, even though she didn't want to admit it. If she'd had a godparent…maybe she would've been saved from some of the perils of her youth.

However, what Miles clearly didn't understand was that, like him, A.J. had a huge family she could rely on, and beyond that, she had two layers of best friends in Caroline and Pepper—three if you counted Margeaux in St. Michel—all of whom A.J. had known longer and were much better choices to care for a child than Sydney. A.J.'s baby would never want for love and care and would certainly never end up in foster care if disaster struck.

She figured it was best to change the subject.

"So all the men on your dad's side of the family are named Miles?" Sydney asked.

He seemed to flinch at the non sequitur.

"Well, not *all* the men." He smiled at her. "All the first-born sons. And for the record, I'm not going to push you to keep talking about the godmother situation, but think about it, okay?"

She nodded, gladly taking him up on the option to change the subject. "And there's been what? Five generations of you?"

"Yes, my birth certificate says Miles Mercer IV."

Sydney narrowed her eyes at him. "I'm just in awe of all this family tradition. Does that mean you'll name your first son accordingly?"

"Unless one of my siblings beats me to the punch," he said. "So far all the grandkids are girls. And since I don't exactly have women standing in line to become Mrs. Miles Mercer IV, they just might beat me to producing the next namesake. But that would be fine because sometimes carrying on a tradition like that feels like more of a burden than an honor."

She wasn't going to get all holier than thou on him, but she couldn't quite ignore the rope of envy that knotted in her belly at the thought of being part of such a large clan. Of course, it was too late for her to ever be a thread in such a tapestry. Some people were just meant to follow different roads. But she could still envy... from afar.

"You said your father was angry at you for the movie," she said. "Why?"

He shifted and she could see a wall go up. "He blames me for dragging the family name through the mud."

"I hate to put it this way, but do you really think your audience cares about family virtue and such? I mean, this is the new millennium; it's not the Victorian era. I did see the movie and I don't think any less of you—except for the fact that I couldn't sleep. I guess I don't understand why he would take it as such an affront."

"Right, I know you had a hard time sleeping." He grinned at her. "You called to let me know, remember?"

Her cheeks warmed at the reminder. She rolled her eyes with the intention of diverting his attention from her embarrassment.

YOUR PARTICIPATION IS REQUESTED!

Dear Reader,

Since you are a lover of romance fiction –
we would like to get to know you!

Inside you will find a short Reader's Survey.
Sharing your answers with us will help our
editorial staff understand who you are and
what activities you enjoy.

To thank you for your participation, we
would like to send you 2 books and 2 gifts –
ABSOLUTELY FREE!

Enjoy your gifts with our appreciation,

Pam Powers

**SEE INSIDE
FOR READER'S
SURVEY**

For Your Romance Reading Pleasure...

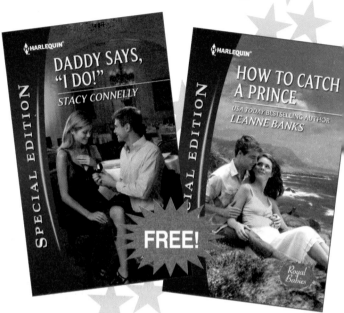

We'll send you 2 books and 2 gifts
ABSOLUTELY FREE
just for completing our Reader's Survey!

YOUR READER'S SURVEY
"THANK YOU" FREE GIFTS INCLUDE:
- ▶ 2 Harlequin® Special Edition books
- ▶ 2 lovely surprise gifts

PLEASE **FILL IN** THE CIRCLES COMPLETELY TO RESPOND

1) What type of fiction books do you enjoy reading? (Check all that apply)
- ○ Suspense/Thrillers ○ Action/Adventure   ○ Modern-day Romances
- ○ Historical Romance ○ Humour   ○ Paranormal Romance

2) What attracted you most to the last fiction book you purchased on impulse?
- ○ The Title   ○ The Cover   ○ The Author   ○ The Story

3) What is usually the greatest influencer when you <u>plan</u> to buy a book?
- ○ Advertising   ○ Referral   ○ Book Review

4) How often do you access the internet?
- ○ Daily ○ Weekly ○ Monthly ○ Rarely or never.

5) How many NEW paperback fiction novels have you purchased in the past 3 months?
- ○ 0 - 2   ○ 3 - 6   ○ 7 or more

YES! I have completed the Reader's Survey. Please send me the 2 FREE books and 2 FREE gifts (gifts are worth about $10) for which I qualify. I understand that I am under no obligation to purchase any books, as explained on the back of this card.

235/335 HDL F5FY

FIRST NAME	LAST NAME

ADDRESS

APT.#	CITY

STATE/PROV.   ZIP/POSTAL CODE

He reached out again and took her hand. The feel of his fingers laced through hers made her skin tingle.

"My dad is all about honor and doing what is right… what *he* thinks is right, that is. In my research, I discovered that my great-great-grandfather's alibi was actually his mistress. He was acquitted for the murder of his wife because he had been with his mistress that night."

"Okay?"

"I reminded everyone of the fact that my great-great-grandfather was an adulterer who had been accused of murdering his wife. Despite the fact that he was found innocent, he was having an affair and my father took issue with that. I guess it made him feel as if we had dredged up all the ghosts of the past again. Especially after another skeleton was discovered just a year before the movie premiered, it probably felt as if the ghost was rearing her head yet again."

"So the legend's ghost is supposedly your great-great-grandmother?"

"So they say."

Sydney nodded. While she didn't agree with extramarital affairs—and she would certainly never want her husband, if she ever married, to carry on with another woman—still…. "An affair really isn't all that shocking, Miles. I mean, sure it's not nice, but when it does happen, it's not a reflection on the entire family. Especially generations down the road."

"That's exactly what I said to my father. We're still barely talking."

"Are you sure there's not more to this that you're not seeing or just not telling me?"

He laughed. It was a dry, humorless sound. "You don't know my dad. The fact that I would air our family's dirty laundry and end up making a career out of it was treason."

His cell phone rang. He pulled it from his pocket and glanced at it. After the second ring, he pushed the button to decline the call, returning it to his pocket.

"Are you up for a little window shopping?" he asked. "I'll take you to my favorite store."

Before Sydney could answer, Miles's phone rang again. He pulled it out again and frowned at the display screen.

"I'm sorry," he said. "I think I should take this."

Sydney nodded. "Of course."

"Hi, Mom, is everything all right?"

His mother. Sydney watched him, feeling a strange sort of heartwarming envy.

"Yes, everything is fine. Nothing to worry about, really."

Sydney didn't mean to eavesdrop. However, since it was nearly three thirty, they were practically the only two in the quiet restaurant and Miles was sitting barely two feet from her. The volume on his phone must have been turned up or maybe his mother simply had one of those full-bodied voices that carried, because she could hear the conversation loud and clear from where she was sitting.

"You've called twice in the last two minutes," Miles said all patience and calm. "I was concerned something was wrong."

"Well, there is sort of an emergency." The words

were muffled, but Sydney could hear the conversation whether she wanted to or not.

Miles sat up in his chair, concern darkening his features.

"Oh, but I don't mean to alarm you, honey. It's not an *emergency* emergency, but I'm kind of in a pickle. I was wondering if you could help me out."

"Sure, Mom. What can I do?"

"Do you remember when I told you that we were allowing Lucy to go to the dance tonight? It's her first real night out since the...*you know what*...the big debacle that we will not mention right now, mainly because there isn't time."

Sydney picked up on the harried and stressed notes in his mother's voice. She also noted the concern etched on Miles's face as he patiently listened. What a contrast to the hardnose he could sometimes be on set.

"Right, Mom, what can I do to help you?"

"Well, I can't find the lipstick I purchased for your sister to wear to the dance tonight. Could you drive into Dallas and pick up a tube of lipstick?"

"What? How is this an emergency?"

Sydney suppressed a smile as she watched Miles rake his hand through his hair and then look at her as he gestured to the phone in disbelief.

"I wouldn't ask if it wasn't very important, honey. She's been so good. She's held up her end of the bargain and I promised her she could have this lipstick if she did certain things. You know, like bring up her grades and stay out of trouble. She held up her end of the bargain beautifully. I can't bear to set a bad example by not holding up my end. I bought the lipstick for her last week, but I stashed it away somewhere and for the life of me, I can't remember where I put it. I just can't let her down after she's been so good."

"Mom, I'm in the middle of something. Lucy won't die if she doesn't have this particular lipstick at this particular moment. Tell her you misplaced it and you'll find it tonight while she's at the dance. At least she gets to go to that and she can have the makeup later."

"Oh. Well…it matches her dress perfectly, and she saved her money to chip in for half the cost. But don't worry about it, sweetie. I suppose I can call your sister Patricia and see if she can swing by on her way home from Aubree's soccer game."

There was no resentment in his mother's voice. Just quiet resignation. At that moment all Sydney could think of was how much she wished she would've grown up in the midst of a big rambunctious brood where someone always needed something and there were half a dozen people you could turn to to help you out when you were in a bind.

Sydney nudged his arm. "Ask her what kind of lipstick."

Miles shot her a quizzical look, and Sydney pointed first to her ear and then toward his cell phone, hoping he got the message that she couldn't help but overhear the conversation.

"Let's go get the lipstick," she said. "Ask her what kind."

He took a deep breath and gave his head a little

shake. Not in refusal, but more in way that seemed to say he thought she was crazy.

She nudged his arm again.

"Okay," he whispered.

"What was that?" his mom asked.

"I said, okay. I'll go get it for you."

"Oh! You're such a sweetheart, Miles. Lucy is almost finished getting her hair done. She has a nail appointment next and there's no way I'd have time to drive all the way to Dallas and back and get her home in time for her date's parents to pick her up."

"Ma, okay, tell me what to get."

"It's MAC lipstick. The shade is called Pretty Please. Now, you'll have to go to one of the nicer department stores to find it. This isn't cheap stuff, but I'll pay you back. It's my fault that the first tube was lost—"

"Ma, wait. So, that's *Mag* lipstick?"

"No, MAC. *M, A, C,*" she spelled.

Sydney whispered, "It's a line of cosmetics. I know what it is."

"I wouldn't know a Mag from a MAC," he said into the phone. "Here, Ma, talk to my friend Sydney. She speaks that language."

He handed a horrified Sydney the phone.

Chapter Eight

Be careful what you wish for because you just might get it, was all Sydney could think as she watched the Mercer family send off Lucy and her date to the dance.

One minute Sydney had been sitting in Bistro St. Germain with Miles, daydreaming about what it would be like to be part of a huge family; a couple of hours later she found herself in the middle of everything.

To say it was a bit overwhelming was the understatement of the year. At certain points—such as when his mother, Deena, began making a big deal out of the fact that Miles had brought a *girl* home—she'd wished she could divert the big brood's attention and quietly slip out into her personal freedom.

Alas, that opportunity had never presented itself, and now, here she stood in the kitchen helping Deena clean up the remnants of the big spaghetti dinner the family had enjoyed after Lucy had left for the dance. The family had insisted that Miles and she stay.

When it's twenty-two people who won't take no for an answer against people who don't quite know where they belong...well, it suffices to say there was strength in numbers.

Plus, it gave her a chance to get a read on this big rift that was dividing Miles and his father. Her preliminary conclusion—at least at first glance—was that the father-and-son relationship wasn't damaged beyond repair.

Miles was playing with nieces, who were hanging off him like little monkeys. He was great with them. He looked so natural.

He'd make a great father someday, and Sydney had a feeling that he just might be the one to give the family their fifth Miles Mercer.

A strange feeling knotted in Sydney's belly. It was an emotion that fell somewhere between longing and regret. She had no idea what it was like to be a sister, niece, daughter or...mother...part of a real family. As she watched him, she put a hand on her stomach as if the gesture could quell the uncomfortable sensation.

"You okay?" asked Deena. "Sometimes spaghetti sauce can upset the system, if you know what I mean. Do you need an antacid, honey?"

"No, thank you, I'm fine, really. Actually, your sauce is *delicious*. In fact, I was going to ask you if you would share your recipe. There's nothing quite like homemade."

Deena began to rattle off a list of ingredients and

how-tos, but then stopped. "I'll write it down for you. Don't let me forget before you leave, okay?"

"That's a deal." She rolled up her sleeves, plunged her hands into the sudsy water and began methodically cleaning the plates, which they had to do in batches since there were so many.

How in the world did Deena live without a dishwasher?

Miles, who had managed to free himself from his adoring nieces, popped into the kitchen.

"Do you two pretty ladies need some help in here?" he asked.

Deena shook her head. "I think we have it all under control. In fact, Sydney, why don't you go on in there and relax with the rest of the family? You've been a big help. I can take it from here."

"I wouldn't dream of leaving you to clean up all alone. It'll go faster if the two of us work on it together."

Miles came and stood between the two of them, putting an arm around both of them. "Then that means it will go even faster if three of us are working on it."

He went to pick up a dish towel to help dry, when the nieces came running into the kitchen.

"Uncle Miles! We're getting ready to start a game of Monopoly. Come play with us!" they said in unison.

"Give me about twenty minutes. I need to help Grandma and Sydney finish cleaning up the kitchen."

They made little-girl protesting noises, the sound that only children who lived a carefree childhood and didn't have to worry about anything more pressing than whether their favorite uncle might join them for a board game could make. The way childhood should be, she thought as she smiled at the way they had resumed hanging on him. He played the part well, stomping around the kitchen acting like some sort of overgrown kid himself.

Then again, he was only twenty-nine, so that wasn't so far-fetched.

"Oh, go in there and play with them, Miles," Deena said. "They don't get to see you enough as it is. I can't have you hiding out in here."

"Would you like to join us?" he asked Sydney.

Sydney shook her head. "Go have fun. I'll join you when we're done."

"Yes, shoo," said Deena. "Go on and get yourself out of here. I'm going to be selfish just this once and keep Sydney in here with me. I want to get to know her better. This is probably one of the few chances I'll get for a little uninterrupted one-on-one time."

Sydney wasn't sure if uninterrupted one-on-one time was a good thing or not. However, it seemed that Deena Mercer didn't have a selfish bone in her body when it came to her kids and grandkids, Sydney mused, as she rinsed and stacked clean plates up for Deena to dry.

"She's a keeper, Miles," Deena said. "Now go on and play."

Sydney felt her face burn scarlet. The woman might not be selfish, but she certainly knew how to embarrass someone. What was she supposed to say to that? Especially when Miles simply smiled and left the kitchen to get in the game with his nieces.

When they were alone again in the kitchen, Deena said, "I really do appreciate you helping me out, hon."

"Like I said, it will go much faster with two of us. I don't know how you manage such a big family without a dishwasher."

Deena laughed. "Actually, what I meant was I'm grateful for how you helped out with Lucy's lipstick. I know Miles would've done it on his own. I didn't realize he was on a date or I wouldn't have asked him in the first place."

A reflex inside Sydney made her want to protest and say it wasn't a date. Especially after how Deena had called her a keeper, but before she could form the words, Deena was telling Sydney the story of how Lucy messed up last year.

Sydney didn't have the heart to interrupt her.

When Deena finally took a breath, Sydney said, "Wow, that could've been serious. I'm glad she was okay."

Deena shook her head. "You know, she was the sweetest, most awkward little thing until she started middle school and she grew boobs. Then all the boys wanted to know her. She's been a challenge, but I suppose this is how she learns. In our family, we have a saying, 'only new mistakes.' It's better that she make the mistakes sooner rather than later when they could be catastrophic."

Sydney watched Deena intently and knew that Lucy was a girl with a strong support system. Lucy was loved and accepted. She'd fallen, but she had landed in this loving, nurturing family's safety net.

Suddenly, Sydney felt every bit like the interloper she was. She could listen and nod. She could even prod a big brother to travel twenty miles to purchase a lipstick reward, but that was where it ended.

It felt very foreign and odd. That hollow feeling of longing and sadness returned. It was the strangest feeling, because in her rational mind, she was happy that the Mercers were such a warm, loving family. But in the broken heart of the scared child that still lived inside her, the little girl who'd never recovered from losing her mother wept for everything she knew she would never have.

That old familiar wall went up. She didn't know why she was so surprised because it always did when she found herself in the midst of a traditional family. She could intellectualize that her family phobia was ridiculous. When she was younger, she thought she could get past it, outgrow the feeling that family was always a "trap." A siren song that promised to always be there. They make you care, they make you trust, and then they leave you.

She realized her mind had been drifting when she saw Deena smiling at her, but she had no idea what she'd said.

So Sydney just smiled back. For the blink of an eye, she wanted to believe in the strength of the family bond and unicorn couples. But then Deena reached out and squeezed Sydney's arm. "Miles likes you. I can tell. I like you, too."

"Yep," said the elder Miles, who was standing in the threshold of a room that was off the kitchen. "I haven't seen him look at a girl the way he looks at you since Julie."

"Who's Julie?" Sydney asked to no one in particular, but neither seemed to hear her. Instead, Deena said, "That's right, Dad. I don't think Miles has even brought home a girl since Julie, has he?"

Dad grunted a "nope," as he walked past them into the family room where the big Monopoly game was going on.

Who was Julie? And what was the significance they seemed to be placing on the fact that Miles hadn't brought home a girl—a *girl?* Had he brought other *women* home since the infamous Julie? She suspected she knew the answer, especially since he said he hadn't been home in five years.

She had to fight the urge to remind them that her visit didn't count. It wasn't a planned meet-the-parents occasion. They were really just delivering Lucy's lipstick. She really wished she hadn't stayed for dinner and she wished that they wouldn't make such a big deal over it.

The thought suddenly had Sydney's throat closing up, and it was difficult for her to breathe. She did her best to smile and managed a squeak that had the semblance of something agreeable before she turned to dry her hands on the blue-and-yellow dish towel that was threaded through the refrigerator door handle.

While her back was turned, she heard Deena say, "Excuse me for just a moment. I'll be right back."

That's when Sydney realized that the activity in the game room had grown mostly silent, except for the sound of Miles and his father arguing.

The elder Miles had said little during dinner and had disappeared into that room off the kitchen after the meal, but now it appeared he was the one doing most of the talking. Until Miles's voice rang above his father's.

He wasn't yelling, but he was firm when he said, "I'm not going to do this tonight, Dad. Not here. Not now. If you want to meet somewhere and talk about this man-to-man like civilized human beings, that would be great. But not now. Instead, we'll say good-night."

Sydney didn't wait for Miles to tell her they were leaving. She set about gathering her purse and exchanging awkward goodbyes and thank-yous. Then they were out the door. Only then was she able to draw in a true, deep breath, one that reached all the way down to the depths of her diaphragm.

They'd been together for nearly twelve hours today, sharing pieces and parts of their lives. He'd shared his family. She'd met the unicorn couple, as unlikely a match as they seemed. Miles believed. For a few very short minutes tonight she'd wanted to believe, too.

Still, after Miles opened the car door for her, settled her in and was on his way around to the driver's side, she exhaled a heavy sigh. With it went all of the remnants of false hope and dreams she might have inadvertently harbored.

Miles likes you. I can tell. I like you, too.

The Mercers were a great family. Miles was strong and sexy and had just enough of a different creative vibe that she could have imagined herself falling for him. Hard.

But Sydney knew better.

When Miles got in the car and looked at her with those eyes that made her insides melt because she wanted to lose herself in them, she forced herself to look away.

The drive to Sydney's house was quiet. They'd spent a lot of time together today. Miles figured they were all talked out. For now.

All in all it had been a great day. Despite the way it had ended as they'd left his parents' house.

Leave it to his dad to drive a pleasant evening into the crapper. As Miles rounded the car to walk Sydney up to her front door, he realized he was grinding his teeth. With that, he resolved he wasn't going to keep venturing into the lion's den. More immediate, he wasn't going to let the guy ruin the rest of his night.

He put his hand on the small of Sydney's back as they walked up the brick path to her door.

He was about to lean in and kiss her when she asked, "So who's Julie?"

He shrugged to hide his confusion. "Julie who?"

"I don't know," she said. "That's why I'm asking. Your mom said I was the first girl you'd brought home since *Julie*. I was just curious to know who she is."

Ah, Julie. That Julie. Sydney didn't sound jealous. In fact, she was smiling and there was a light tone to her voice.

"She was my high school girlfriend. I haven't thought about her in ages."

"I figured as much," Sydney said. "I mean that she

was an old girlfriend. But high school? Really? You haven't brought anyone home since?"

"You saw my family," he said. "They can be a little over the top. They're certainly not for the faint of heart."

She smiled. "I've never really experienced that kind of togetherness. But they're wonderful, Miles. You're lucky to have them. Even your dad. Speaking of, what are you going to do about that situation?"

"I have no idea. Except that right now, I know I don't want him to ruin the rest of our night."

He leaned in and kissed her soft and slow, tracing the lush fullness of her bottom lip with his tongue. When she slipped her hands around his neck, his body reacted to the taste and feel of her.

As he pulled her in closer, he felt her stiffen and pull back slightly.

"Are you okay?" he asked.

"I am. It's been a wonderful day, but it's getting late."

He brushed a gentle kiss on her forehead.

"Why don't we have a glass of wine and tell me what other secrets my mother spilled tonight?"

"Well, if they're secrets, I can't tell you," she said. "I would ask you to come in, but tomorrow I have to finish contacting the brides who are finalists on the show and confirm the time we can meet them on Monday. So I'd better call it a night."

"What do you mean you're working tomorrow?"

"Someone has to get everything lined up so that everything goes smoothly on Monday."

He leaned in and rested his forehead on hers.

"You're smart, beautiful and dedicated, too," he said.

"Yeah, well, tell Lenny to give me a raise for all this dedication." This time, she brushed his lips with a kiss.

Again, his body responded to the sheer proximity of her and it took every ounce of strength he had to keep from picking her up and carrying her to her bed and showing her just how well she did it for him. "Ooh, I could make some very off-color comments about who is giving who a raise right about now," he said.

She laughed and then was suddenly sober.

"You realize if we ever do…" Her voice trailed off for a moment. "It would only be a fling because I may be moving to St. Michel, and even if I don't you're eventually going back to L.A. So, maybe it's best if we don't start something we can't finish?"

"I think it's too late for that. I think we've passed that point where we could've walked away a long time ago."

Miles kissed her so thoroughly that it made her toes curl in her sandals. It took everything Sydney had not to invite him inside.

Instead, she said good-night and went inside alone.

If she'd invited him in, she knew where things would end up. If they ended up *there,* she'd be a goner. If it was possible to be farther gone than she already was.

Tonight, he wasn't her boss or the hotshot Hollywood director. He'd been *real.* Beloved son, ideal uncle… the understudy for the role of perfect father…he fit the role perfectly. Sydney could recognize that from a mile away.

He was meant to be a father—and he wanted kids

someday. There was not a chance in hell that she would ever have children.

She sighed at the realization of just how deep the layers were that made their situation so impossible, set her handbag on the living room chair and turned on the lamp. The air conditioner clicked on and the cool air blew down on her making her feel cold…and very alone in this empty house.

If imagined ghosts had haunted her last night, tonight a very real demon had lodged itself in her heart, making it ache for the impossibility of the situation.

What in the world was she going to do? This was a slippery slope she was standing on. If she were wise, she would take a big step back and put some much-needed distance between them. But common sense and her heart were at war with one another.

She stepped out of the air draft, hugging herself to ward off the chill that had settled in her bones despite the summer humidity that had wrapped around them like a blanket as they said good-night on the porch.

She'd just stepped into the kitchen to brew herself a cup of herbal tea when she noticed the blinking light on the answering machine.

She pressed the button and walked over to the sink to fill the kettle.

"Hello, I am calling for Madam Sydney James." She turned off the tap at the sound of the accented voice. "Madam James, I am very pleased to inform you that you are one of two candidates we have selected for the next round of interviews for the St. Michel press secretary position. We will be conducting final interviews here in St. Michel during the time of the Royal Anniversary festival. You will participate in a working interview helping to promote the anniversary festival so that we might see how you conduct yourself on the job. We will be in touch shortly with specific details. In the meantime, please be prepared to arrive in St. Michel in about three weeks."

If she'd asked the heavens to give her a sign about whether or not to get involved with Miles, this was about as clear as an engraved missive providing her with detailed directions for the distance she so desperately needed to keep herself from falling for him any more than she already had.

Chapter Nine

Sydney decided the best approach was to be direct. As soon as she got to work the next morning, she texted A.J., Caroline and Pepper and asked if they could have a quick meeting before they started the day's taping.

Actually, her text was more of the "Coffee in my office?" variety because if she'd said "Quick meeting in my office?" they would've started asking questions. She didn't want to discuss this through text messages. Really, she didn't want to do this at all, face-to-face was the lesser of the evils.

She had to tell them that she was a finalist for the job in St. Michel before she told anyone else, namely Miles. They were her friends and business partners. Now that there was a very real possibility that she would be leaving the show—and be an absentee business partner—

she owed them a straight answer. And they deserved to hear it first, before anyone else.

When they all had their coffee and were gathered in her office, a knot, cold and leaden, formed in the pit of her stomach. It struck her that they'd happily come in early just to have coffee in her office.

This was going to be more difficult than she'd bargained for. That's why it was tempting to let the chit-chat continue without interruption.

That is until Pepper turned the subject to Miles. "So give us the update. How did the date go?"

She remembered the feel of his mouth on hers and crossed her arms as if that could provide protection from the longing he stirred in her.

As if.

She traced her bottom lip with one of her fingers.

"It was great. A little overwhelming. I met the entire family."

"What?" Pepper exclaimed. "Tell us *everything*."

Suddenly, three pair of eager eyes were trained on her. Sydney's nervous gaze skittered to the clock on her computer screen. They were supposed to report to hair and makeup in fifteen minutes. Did she really want to break the news now?

No, actually, she didn't.

Still, it wasn't going to get any easier as time went on. It pretty much felt like now or never, which, for a split second, made her question whether she really wanted to leave if it was *that* hard to share the news about the job interview.

Of course she wanted the job. Frankly, a reality show

like *Catering to Dallas* had a shelf life, and that expiration date would be here sooner than she'd like to believe. Jobs like the St. Michel press secretary position didn't come along every day. It was time to go.

That didn't mean she wouldn't keep in touch. It just meant that it was time to go.

"Hey, Syd, are you with us?" A.J. asked, snapping Sydney out of her thoughts.

"Actually," she said, purposely not elaborating on her answer to the question about Miles, "I may *not* be with you much longer. That's why I asked you to meet me this morning." She took a deep breath and said the words before she lost her nerve. "I have a job interview in St. Michel. I'm one of two finalists for the position of press secretary to the royal family."

Three pair of eyes were still riveted on her, only this time they looked as if they were waiting for the punch line to a joke they couldn't quite figure out.

Sydney held her breath while her friends digested the news.

"You can't be serious," said Caroline. "We're right in the middle of taping the show. You can't just—" she shook her head "—*leave us*. We need you."

We need you.

Why did Caroline have to say it like that? Sydney knew breaking the news wouldn't be easy, but she had no idea it would be this difficult.

The look on the girls' faces as realization dawned was nothing short of heartbreaking.

Time for damage control.

Putting a proper spin on something unpleasant was

what Sydney did. It was where she excelled. However, at the moment, it seemed that the words she needed to make this easier escaped her. Maybe it was because Caroline's words still seemed to echo in the air.

We need you.

"You don't need me," she finally said. "In fact, you won't even miss me. Not on *Catering to Dallas*. Of course, I'll remain a silent partner in Celebrations, Inc. That is, if that arrangement works for everyone. But we're getting ahead of ourselves. It's just an interview. They haven't offered me the job. I simply felt like I should tell you before the interview."

"Yet," spat Pepper. "They haven't offered you the job *yet*. Of course they will. Unless they're idiots."

"Well, thank you…I think?" Suddenly, Sydney's office seemed unbearably stuffy and close. She wished she could step out into the hall and reclaim her equilibrium. She hadn't felt this off-kilter since the day she'd learned she was losing her job at Texas Star Energy, the company that had brought her from St. Michel to Celebration, Texas, in the first place. Of course, the layoff had turned out to be a blessing in disguise because Texas Star ultimately crumbled under the weight of a financial scandal. Sydney had narrowly escaped getting caught up in the red tape. And though obviously she'd had no knowledge of the underhanded deals that bilked thousands of people out of millions of dollars, it still felt personal—both the layoff and the company's demise. She'd felt utterly betrayed and out of control.

How ironic. Now she was the one in control and allowing herself the option of completing the circle by moving back to St. Michel.

For someone who was so *in control,* why did she feel as if she were coming unglued?

She cleared her throat. "When Texas Star failed and I came on board here at Celebrations, Inc., it was only supposed to be a temporary thing. Remember? I was up-front with you about the fact that I wasn't sure how long I'd stay in Texas since my place at Texas Star had fallen through. I need to ensure my future and my livelihood. And really, Celebration, Texas, isn't my home."

Her voice cracked on the word *home,* and she had to swallow hard to maintain her composure.

Where was her home? She braced herself for one of them to ask her that very question and remind her that Celebration was the closest thing to *home* that she'd ever known. These three women were the closest thing to family she'd ever had. Instead, they stared at her in apparent disbelief that made Sydney's heart ache and had her questioning herself: why *was* she leaving? She couldn't ignore the small voice inside her that asked the question.

But she had answers, and she trotted them out one by one as she reminded herself that this was what she needed to do, even if she really didn't want to do it.

Even though her friends had become more like sisters in the three years she'd known them, *this* wasn't the life she wanted. Even at thirty-five, she still longed to find someone to share her life with. That might not mean marriage or a traditional relationship like her friends enjoyed. She might never settle down in that manner, but she wanted a nontraditional man who was happy to be her life mate, one who understood her restless spirit and was willing to explore uncharted waters with her.

They may think they wanted her to stay, but once her friends started having children—and for A.J., that was only a few weeks away—their lives would change drastically. They'd get caught up in diapers and play dates and T-ball teams and carpools. She didn't want to be the fifth wheel, the honorary auntie, the hanger-on who everyone speculated about: Why doesn't your friend Sydney find a nice man and get married and settle down? Doesn't she want kids?

Miles's face flashed in her mind. That familiar ache fed by the impossibility of the situation made her heart hurt. She ran her tongue over her bottom lip and tasted phantom shades of his kiss. If she let herself get more emotionally involved with him than she already was, it was only a recipe for heartbreak.

"You have to understand that I'm single. I'm on my own. You have your husbands and families. I have to make sure I make choices that will ensure my own future security. Despite how much fun we're having right now, we all know that *Catering to Dallas* isn't going to last forever. I have to think about my future and it seems to be pointing toward St. Michel."

"But what about the *Single Ladies* cookbook?" Pepper asked. "I have a feeling that's going to be big. That could be your future."

Sydney had to bite the insides of her cheeks to keep from pointing out the horrible irony of her statement.

Sydney James, forever branded the *Single Lady*. While that was probably truer than she'd like to admit—after all, she really didn't want to get married—she didn't want it permanently tattooed on her forehead. Not even in the metaphorical sense.

"Pepper, I love your enthusiasm," she said. "And I hope the cookbook does well, too, but I can't turn down what might be the opportunity of a lifetime for something that is so uncertain."

Pepper frowned and remained uncharacteristically quiet, which reinforced the fact that this was the right move, no matter how difficult its realities.

A.J. folded her hands atop her basketball belly.

"Is that why you've been so hesitant to commit to being my standby Lamaze coach?" she asked.

Wow. They really weren't going to make this easy on her, were they?

"Yes," Sydney admitted. "I didn't want to promise something I couldn't deliver. If I'm in St. Michel when you go into labor, there's no guarantee that I'll get here in time. That's not fair to you and the baby. I didn't want to say anything about the job possibility until I knew whether I was one of the final candidates."

"That's fair," A.J. answered, but her expression suggested that she wasn't happy about it. "But, Syd, the distance shouldn't have any bearing on whether or not you're the baby's godmother."

Oh, boy. Here we go.

"Except, wouldn't it be unfair to the child if I lived a continent away? Shouldn't a baby have a godmother who is part of her life?"

"No, it wouldn't be unfair," said A.J. "Being a godmother is really more a symbol of commitment, a promise to always be there." A.J.'s lower lip quivered. For a moment, Sydney thought her friend might cry, but then she said, "How are you ever going to have this future you're so desperately seeking if you're too afraid to put down roots?"

A.J.'s words harkened back to what Maya had asked when Sydney was in St. Michel for the first round of interviews: *What are you running from?*

Of course, Maya had also said, *True friends would be happy for you. They wouldn't hold you back from your path. Unless you don't believe this is your path?*

As she looked from one face to another, Sydney knew she wasn't certain it was the right path. But the opportunity was calling. If she stayed here, she'd remain stuck in the no-man's-land of doing a job that Pepper was much better equipped to handle—at least in this market, where she was much more socially connected. In all her restless years when she'd moved from place to place, Sydney had always believed she'd recognize what she was looking for when she found it.

"There you are." Miles appeared in the threshold of Sydney's office, and her breath caught at the sight of him. "Okay, what's going on in here? It feels like someone died. Is everyone okay?"

"He obviously doesn't know," Pepper said.

"I don't know *what?*" he asked, casting a wary glance at Sydney.

"I think this is our cue to leave, girls," said Caroline. "We need to go to hair and makeup anyway."

She reached out and squeezed Sydney's shoulder. "Whatever happens, you know we'll support you," she said. "That's what friends do."

"Of course we will," A.J. said.

Both she and Pepper hugged Sydney before they slipped past Miles.

Then it was just the two of them, standing face-to-face, with unspoken words hanging in the air like a question mark.

"I didn't mean to interrupt," Miles said. He wanted to kiss her good-morning, and he would have if not for this *wall* he sensed between them. Obviously, it was a wall built of whatever she wasn't telling him.

"It's okay," she said. "You're not interrupting."

He fingered the piece of paper he was holding.

"Here, this is for you." He handed her the paper. She took it and glanced at it. "My mom's marinara recipe. She emailed it to me. She said she meant to give it to you before we left, but I guess we beat a pretty hasty exit. Was my family too much? I hope they didn't scare you off because I would really love to see you again."

He'd learned that the best approach was the direct approach. He'd given her her space yesterday, but she'd occupied his every waking thought. She'd lived in the recesses of his thoughts even when his mind was trained on something else. There was this space inside of him that she'd carved out where she'd taken up permanent residence.

"Your family is wonderful, Miles," she said. "It was

a privilege to meet them. Tell your mom I said thank you for the recipe. I can't wait to try it."

"I'll do that," he said. "But first tell me what's going on?"

She nodded, but she wouldn't look at him. He followed her gaze to the framed Audrey Hepburn poster that dominated one wall of her tiny office.

"I got a callback for the job," she said. "I'm one of two finalists for the position. I had to tell Pepper, Caroline and A.J. first because they're my business partners. I felt like I owed it to them to tell them first."

"I understand," he said, even though his mind was racing to figure out exactly what that meant for the show. And for them.

"I was going to tell you later."

His timing was obviously off. That seemed to be a problem lately—meeting her now when she was poised to move a continent away.

He'd met a lot of beautiful women in his lifetime, but none had the certain something that drew him to Sydney.

"Congratulations." He managed a genuine smile. "I knew you'd get the callback. When is the interview?"

"Thank you, Miles." Those three words seemed to be filled with such relief that she finally felt like herself again. Especially when she stepped closer and hugged him. Still in his arms, she tilted her chin up to look at him. "I leave in three weeks. They're having the other finalist and me come in to help with the Royal Anniversary Festival. It will be a working interview."

"A working interview for what?" Lenny stood in

the threshold of the office, one beefy arm braced on the door frame.

Miles and Sydney took a step away from each other. Miles looked to Sydney to tell Lenny as much as she wanted to disclose.

"Don't keep me in the dark," Lenny persisted. "Tell me what's going on."

"I have a job interview," she said matter-of-factly. Miles loved her no-nonsense strength, especially with Lenny. Lenny was a ballbuster and did his damnedest to intimidate people. It never worked with Sydney.

"What do you mean you have a job interview? Your job is here. You have a contract."

"Lenny, this isn't just an average, run-of-the-mill job possibility."

She explained how she was one of two finalists for the St. Michel press secretary post and how she hadn't gone looking for the job; they had come to her.

"That's the place where they discovered the long-lost princess, right? That woman from the States who had no idea she was royalty, right?"

Sydney nodded.

"Is she a friend of yours or something?" Lenny asked.

Again, Sydney nodded, then immediately shot Miles a glance that said she regretted telling him.

Rightfully so.

"So, I guess that means that you're pretty much a shoo-in for the job," Lenny said.

The wheels in Lenny's head were obviously turning. The guy was so transparent. Sydney and Miles exchanged another glance.

"Well, no," Sydney finally said. "I'm not *guaranteed* the job. I have to go through the paces like everyone else. They will choose whoever they feel is the best candidate for the position. Whoever will best serve the royal family and the government."

"And you're BFFs with the queen," Lenny snarked. "Yeah. So enough said. No contest. The job is yours, sweetheart. There's no need for pretense here. We're your friends, too. Since we are such good buddies, I'll cut you a deal. When you get the job, I'll let you out of your *Catering to Dallas* contract scot-free on one condition. You let our crew follow you on the interview as you're going through these pretend paces working the Royal Anniversary Celebration. Isn't that what you said you have to do? Don't worry, we'll make it look legit. No one will know it's fake and fixed."

Miles had never seen Sydney pull such a face. For a minute, he thought she was going to deck Lenny.

"No." The word packed a firmer punch than a heavyweight fighter could've thrown.

"No?" Lenny mocked. "What do you mean, *no?*"

Sydney put her hands on her hips. "It means exactly what you know it means, Lenny. *No.* Even if the government of St. Michel would grant you permission to film the process—allow you to come inside the castle and nose around the private quarters of the family and staff—there's no way I would ever let you follow me. This is a job interview, Lenny. Bringing my own camera crew would be unprofessional, not to mention it would be in very bad taste."

"Don't be ridiculous. It would be a boon for a PR person to get a national television show to film something like the Royal Anniversary Celebration. You're going to be dealing with media, anyway. Why not throw a bone to the ones who gave you your start? Give us the exclusive."

Sydney's face flushed scarlet. Somehow Miles knew that all she wanted to do was leave the confines of the office, but Lenny was blocking the doorway with his behemoth cattleman's frame.

"Lenny," Miles said, "Sydney's right. It's not appropriate. It would put undue pressure on Sydney in an already stressful situation. Besides, even if she and the powers that be in St. Michel were willing to let you follow her, the budget won't allow us to load up the crew on such short notice and trek over to Europe. Sydney, isn't it time for you to go to hair and makeup? Lenny, you might want to let her out so that we don't get behind schedule."

Chapter Ten

"I didn't get a chance to say this earlier, but I really appreciate how you handled Lenny this morning," Sydney said as they got into Miles's car to go interview the third candidate for the *Celebration's Bride* special.

Miles slanted a wry smile at her as he eased the car onto the highway. "He's full of good ideas, isn't he?"

"He's full of something, but I don't know if it's good ideas."

They both laughed.

She reached out and put her hand on his arm, loving the way his hard muscles felt under her fingers. She had a sudden urge to smooth the hair on his tanned skin and slide her hand down into his to see if their fingers still fit together as perfectly as she remembered. Instead, she took her hand away and put it in her lap.

"Seriously, I appreciate you having my back," she said.

He nodded and turned on the radio. Notes of a soul-ful blues song spilled out into the empty space between them. They rode without speaking, listening to the guy sing, "Baby, please don't go." She watched him as he drove, taking advantage of the opportunity to drink him in. His square jaw was covered by a fresh crop of whiskers that had grown in during the day. He'd been clean-shaven this morning, but it was after five o'clock now and the sexy shadow that had sprouted during the day lent him a sexy air that was part dangerous and all man. His lips were not exceptionally full—more like just right. She had the sudden urge to taste them again. He was quite a guy, strong enough to stand up for what he believed in, yet he had enough heart to not let his views stand between him and what really mattered…his family.

He was the kind of guy who, when he talked, people listened—people like Lenny who usually didn't have enough sense to back away from a rattlesnake.

Miles had defended her today. He'd stood up for her, and that made him even sexier than his great looks. Or maybe it added to them.

When was the last time someone had really gone to bat for her?

She sighed and entwined her hands to keep from reaching out and touching him again.

"I'm sorry you had to find out about my interview the way you did. I did feel like I owed it to A.J., Caro-line and Pepper to tell them first."

He stopped in front of the bride's house, turned off

the car and looked over at her. "I understand. But I'm not going to lie. I wish you weren't leaving. I know it's selfish of me to say that because it's a great opportunity for you, but I just can't help but think about how screwed up the timing of everything is. It's been a long time since I've met anyone I've been this attracted to and now you're getting ready to move to another continent."

His words took her breath away, and she wasn't sure what to say. Actually, she wasn't sure she could speak. Miles's gaze snared hers as he opened his door. There was a tingling in the pit of her stomach, and she could feel the magnetism that made him so self-confident. It radiated from him in waves that were almost palpable.

"Hold that thought," she said as she opened her own door. "We'll finish that conversation as soon as we're finished with our bride."

"I'm looking forward to it," he said.

"I'm so glad y'all are here," Lily Palmer said as she welcomed them into her modest home. She was the third of three candidates for *Catering to Dallas's Celebration's Bride* contest.

Miles had let Sydney and her business partners choose the three finalist candidates from the thousands of letters they'd received after they'd aired the call for entries. Lenny and Aiden had to sign off on the choices, of course.

Once that was signed and sealed, Miles had agreed to go along on the initial interviews to check out the brides' homes and surroundings for taping purposes.

The first finalist they visited was a nurse who looked in on geriatric patients on her days off; the second candidate was a violinist who gave free music lessons to underprivileged kids.

Now here they sat in the modest living room of Lily Henderson, a schoolteacher who had started a program to ensure every child in her school received a hot lunch. Lily had also made sure Miles and Sydney didn't go hungry during their visit. She'd prepared a feast of sweets for them, which she'd arranged on platters on the living room table.

"I stayed up all night baking for y'all," she said. "So please eat. How do you take your coffee? Or would you prefer tea? The water is ready. All I have to do is get the teabag."

"I'd love a cup of tea," Sydney said. "Thank you so much."

"As soon as I heard your British accent, I figured you might," Lily said. "I'll be right back. Miles? What can I get for you?"

"I'll have coffee. Black, please."

"Isn't she adorable?" Sydney said as soon as Lily was out of the room.

She was nice enough and would work well for the show, Miles thought, but he only had eyes for one woman and she was sitting right next to him.

Sydney smiled at him and he realized at that moment that he would move mountains for this woman. He planned to tell her so when they picked up their to-be-continued conversation after they left Lily's.

His phone buzzed, signaling an incoming text. He glanced at it. It was a message from his little sister Lucy:

Have you decided whether or not you can come speak to my class for career day? I'm really counting on you.

He must've been frowning because Sydney asked, "Is everything okay?"

"Nothing earth shattering," he said. "It's just Lucy. She wants me to be a speaker at her school's career day."

Sydney cocked her head to the side. "Why wouldn't you? I'm sure you'd be a big hit with the kids and that would automatically qualify you for big-brother-hero status with your sister. Why the hesitation?"

He shook his head. "That's how it would be in a perfect world, but of course nothing is that simple. My father has his heart set on speaking, telling about his days in the army. Once a military man, always a military man, and he can't resist the opportunity to recruit a young 'un into the service. I'm trying to find out if Lucy can bring two guests. If not, I'd better bow out and let the old man have his day. According to my mom, he's been planning his talk for weeks."

Sydney's mouth formed an O.

Then Lily came back in with a tray complete with cups, saucers, a coffeepot, another china pot with warm water for Sydney's tea, cream, sugar and lemon wedges.

"I forgot to ask you how you wanted your tea," Lily said. "So I went ahead and brought out all the fixings."

"Thank you," Sydney said, as she added a splash of

cream to her tea. "This is exactly how I like it. Your tea and coffee service is gorgeous. Where did you get it?"

Lily settled herself in the chair across from the couch where they sat. Her legs were crossed primly at the ankle, her hands clasped on the skirt of her brightly flowered dress.

"It belonged to my grandmother," she said. "She raised me after both of my parents passed away. Car accident," she added with a solemn dip of her head, as if answering the question of what happened before it was even asked had become a rote response. "She passed away about a month ago and that and the house are all I have left of her. I didn't realize it until after she was gone, but she'd taken out a second mortgage on this house to put me through college. I never would've let her do that if I'd known. She always said she didn't want me to worry about having to work while I was going to school." Suddenly, Lily's fingers fluttered to her mouth.

"Listen to me just blabbing away. I'm so sorry. I'm sure you didn't come here to listen to my tales of woe. So let me just say, I would be very honored and grateful if I were selected as Celebration's Bride because the cash prize would not only give my fiancé, Josh, and me a chance to have our dream wedding, but it would help me pay off a little of the debt on this house."

She blinked at them sheepishly. "Please have some of the cookies. I promise I'll quit blathering on and on. I'm sure you have a lot to tell me about the contest."

Miles picked up a plate and handed it to Sydney. She thanked him and helped herself to a chocolate cookie and a small sweet that was either a spongy cookie or a small cake. Miles stood to hand a plate to Lily.

"Oh, no thank you," she said. "I love to bake—it's my stress release—but I've promised myself and Josh that I won't eat a single sweet until we feed each other our wedding cake. You see, I found my dress on sale, but it was a size too small. But it really was my dream dress. I figured they could let it out as much as the seams will allow and I can lose weight—because I need to, anyway—and it will fit."

She sighed and looked longingly at the array of sweets on the table. "Do they taste okay? Usually I taste everything before I serve it, but I have to keep my no-sweets promise to Josh. He doesn't want a fat wife."

That was a little harsh, Miles thought.

But Lily giggled and that gave him hope that maybe "doesn't want a fat wife" was Lily's interference and not her fiancé's words.

Sydney set down plate on her lap. "Everything is delicious. How much weight have you lost? Because you look fine to me."

"Well, thank you." Lily beamed at them. "I'm not sure. Our bathroom scale is broken. I didn't replace it because I read something that said you should throw out your scale and simply go by how your clothes feel." She tugged at the side seam of her flowered dress. "This is one of my favorite dresses and it feels great, but then again, the material has a little give to it, which is nice for when I'm in the classroom. But I guess I'll know soon enough when I go in for my next fitting."

The woman was a talker. But better a talker than not

for the show. She was so different from Sydney, but he had a feeling Sydney felt a connection with Lily. They had both been orphaned as children. Miles imagined Sydney might lean more toward her than the other two contestants.

Miles glanced at Sydney and wondered how things might have been different for her if she'd had a grandmother to rely on rather than being shuttled through the foster-care system. But Sydney's background—as flawed as it might be—was what made her the strong, fiercely independent woman for whom Miles had fallen so hard. At that moment, as he sat there listening to Sydney ask Lily questions about her life, job, fiancé and their future, he wished he could be the one to give Sydney the life she'd missed out on. Even though nothing could change the past, there was always the future.

Chapter Eleven

It was after seven o'clock when they left Lily's house. Miles had insisted on taking Sydney to dinner to celebrate her good news about the job interview.

He'd ordered a bottle of champagne and toasted her success. He was being so wonderful about it. Actually, if he'd sat down and strategized a plan to seduce her he couldn't have done a better job. She wanted him, and everything that was genuine and true compelled her to show him.

As they sat in the car in front of her house, each time she looked at him, the magnetic pull was stronger. Then, impulsively, she leaned over and planted a feather-light kiss on his lips.

"Thank you," she said. "And not just for dinner. For everything. For being on my side…for being you."

Miles sat very still and sucked in a breath. An ominous light smoldered in his dark brown eyes. Sydney knew she was playing with fire, but she couldn't stop herself. She cupped his face in her hands, leaned in again and went in for a real kiss this time.

The happenings of the past couple of days—meeting Miles and his family, getting the call about the job, talking to this fabulous bride-to-be who'd made her believe maybe, just maybe, there was such a thing as happily ever after—made her realize that it wasn't going to be as easy to leave as she thought it would be. But she wasn't going to think about that right now or everything else that had happened recently. Each event heaped another emotion on top of the one that came before it, making everything feel electric and volatile like a brewing tempest.

Judging by the look on Miles's face, this was the calm before spark that just might blow her carefully laid plans sky-high.

As she deepened the kiss, Miles growled deep in his throat, and she knew she was right. Because suddenly, he was kissing her back.

Kissing her hard. Holding her face in place with his palms firmly on her cheeks and his fingers tangled in her hair. He was moving his lips over hers so ravenously, even if she'd wanted to resist, she couldn't. But she didn't want to.

Slowly, he pulled back and stared down at her. "Are you sure this is what you want?"

Self-preservation urged her to say no, but the word wouldn't pass her lips no matter how she tried to force it. Even though she couldn't form the words, she knew she could no more walk away from what was about to happen than she could stop breathing.

She felt his breath against her hot lips, saw the voracious hunger that deepened the intensity of his brown eyes. She warned herself to be smart, to stop this while she could.

Instead, she heard herself saying, "Yes. Kiss me."

A desperate kind of need clenched in her stomach, and the fact that she wanted him so much floored her.

"I'll kiss you," he said, and it sounded more like a warning than a promise. "But I can't promise that's where it will end. Stop me now if this is not what you want."

She answered him with a kiss of her own. He responded with a take-no-prisoners reaction. His mouth was forceful and a little rough. He pulled her across the console onto his lap. She knocked into the gearshift and steering wheel and everything else that stood between them. But that didn't stop the intense frenzy of kisses—mouth to mouth, mouth to neck, hands fisting in hair, tugging at clothing so that they could be skin to skin.

His tongue thrust into her mouth and he slid his hands around to grip her bottom and direct her hips in a rhythm that moved her against his rock-hard erection. She shuddered as lightning flashed from her heart to the taut, throbbing core between her legs.

"I think we better go inside," he murmured through a kiss. "Or we're going to be the talk of the neighborhood."

She wrapped her arms around his neck and sank into his chest. "The neighbors. They're such a bother."

They walked to her door hand in hand. When they were inside, Miles picked her up and carried her into the bedroom.

"How did you know which one was my room?" she asked.

"Good instincts." His lips closed around hers, eclipsing the words, and he gently lowered her onto the bed. He stretched out on top of her. Entwining their fingers, he swept their arms upward, until they were extended overhead, their linked fingers a symbol of two becoming one. Then he found her mouth and bestowed long, leisurely, soul-stirring kisses that melted her bones and set fire to the blood in her veins. She realized the appreciative little hum she heard was coming from deep in her throat, a response to his kisses and the weight of his body pressing her into the mattress.

He caught her lower lip in his mouth and tugged at it with his teeth. He released it, then he raised up to look at her.

"Are you sure this is what you want?"

She looked up at him through the hazy glow of want.

"I can't think of anything I've wanted more."

With a kiss to seal the deal, he tugged her red blouse over her head, rewarding her with open-mouthed kisses, which he dragged down her throat. She almost got lost in the sheer pleasure of it all, but at least had enough of her wits about her to follow suit and free him of his shirt so that they could finally lay skin to skin.

The contact heated Sydney's blood to a rolling boil.

She was greedy for the feel of him. She ran her hands up his arms and across his shoulders. She sketched his collarbone with her fingertips.

As she fanned out her fingers over his chest, Miles undid the button on her slacks and pulled down the zipper. She arched toward him and he pulled the garment off, leaving her in nothing but her matching red bra and tiny lace panties.

She hooked her fingers in the waistband of his pants and tugged. He made short order of freeing himself from the last of his clothes. As he did, she saw him fumbling with his wallet. He took out a small foil packet and tossed it onto the bedside table.

She was glad he had a condom. She wasn't on birth control and the last thing she wanted was to get pregnant.

He sprawled out on top of her, raking his fingers through her hair, pushing it back away from her face, before he captured her lips again with his.

The wall of resistance Sydney had built up crumbled to dust as he dominated her with his mouth, his tongue, his body. She was vaguely aware of the humming sounds that were once again reverberating in her throat, but she ignored them, returning his ravenous kisses with an appetite of her own.

They clung to each other with lips and hands and arms and legs. Skin to skin wasn't close enough. Their bodies bucked to be as close as possible. The feel of him drove her to the edge of control. That almost gave her pause, because all of her cognizant life had been built around maintaining control. She pulled back, searching through the haze of arousal for her emotional armor.

"Trust me," he whispered as if he'd read her mind.

"I will… I do…" She hated feeling so vulnerable, but she didn't know how to tell him.

Perhaps the lesson she was learning now was that control was overrated.

He gazed down at her bee-stung lips and her amorous eyes, which had darkened to the color of deep jade. "It's okay. Trust me?"

She nodded.

He dipped his head and nipped at the soft skin at the juncture of her neck and the curve of her jaw. Sydney sucked in a breath. Shuddering, she raised her chin, providing him better access.

She fisted her hands into his hair, reveling in the pleasure. He liked to see her let down her guard.

His fingers cupped her breast, reaching into her bra to circle her nipple with his index finger. He caught her nipple between his thumb and finger, lightly pinching it until she sucked in a breath that hissed through her teeth.

He unhooked the front clasp of her bra and freed her gorgeous breasts. They were creamy pale orbs that sat high and boasted lush bottomed curves. Miles leaned down to capture one in his mouth.

He looked up at her and saw the ecstasy in her green eyes. Holding her gaze, he sucked on her nipple, working his tongue in a circular motion.

Air burst out of her lungs in a sudden gasp.

He hooked his fingers in her panties and tugged them down. He rolled onto his side, retrieved the condom from the bedside table, ripped it open and rolled it down the length of his erection.

He stationed himself above her, bowing his head to kiss her and to rub his chest against her breasts.

Instinctively, her fingers found the base of his penis and she guided it to her opening. Miles nudged forward with his hips and sank into her. She shifted her legs, drawing her knees up to meet him thrust for thrust.

A soft moan escaped her lips and he took that as his cue to pick up speed until Sydney sighed with satisfaction.

He was so close. So. Very. Close. But he didn't want this to be over just yet. Not until she'd had her fill. Miles slipped his hand between their bodies, searching for the soft rise of her mound. He located the bud of her womanhood with his fingertip. Sydney let out a strangled cry.

It had been a long time since a man had taken her to such great heights. As he sank into her again and again and again, Sydney realized she could be very content staying in bed with Miles for the foreseeable future. He was a master at lovemaking, finding spots that she'd never known existed on her body. He had her pleading for more.

She peered up at him and he flashed her a crooked smile.

"You are something else, Sydney. You are so special, you make me lose my words."

She lifted a finger to his lips. "Then don't speak. *Show me.*"

With that, he swiveled his hips, pulled back and then thrust deep into her again and again and again. Moving with a purpose, seeking the apex that was just out of her reach, she looked up to his face. He looked ethereal, like equal parts archangel and tormentor. He was probably a mixture of the two. He was definitely the one who was in control. The way he made her feel, she was more than happy to let him pluck the strings that made her dance.

She pleaded for him to drive her over the edge, and responded by moving faster and faster and faster, until the friction ignited the fuse inside her that exploded like Hollywood special effects as shockwaves of pure, untainted rapture shocked her body.

Even in the midst of her own orgasm, she was fully aware of Miles driving deep into her for the final time and of his deep groan of pleasure in tandem with her own breathless satisfaction as she fought to catch her breath.

Miles collapsed on top of her, and she wrapped her arms around his broad back and welcomed the warmth and weight of him. She felt limp and languid, as if she were a cottony dandelion blossom that would break apart and float into the stratosphere. She had never felt so spent and relaxed in her life.

Until carnal ecstasy began to subside and reality seeped into the cracks of her mosaic heart.

She smoothed her hands over Miles's broad back and

tried to fight off the thoughts that were jeering at her, reminding her that this was a mistake.

Not because she didn't feel anything for Miles. *Au contraire.* She already felt too much for him.

Sometimes she was her own worst enemy.

She felt his hot breath on her neck, the smooth skin of his tanned back and felt herself begin to slip down that slippery slope. Because despite how her rational mind was still demanding to know *what the hell she'd done,* she would've been lying if she said she didn't want to hold him in her arms, just like this, for a very long time.

Yet the interview was in three weeks and he'd be leaving shortly after this. She knew she had no business thinking of a future for the two of them.

If they were going to be together, it meant that someone would have to compromise. She'd learned from experience: compromise bred resentment.

Good Lord, what had she done?

Chapter Twelve

Miles had always been a realist, but over the next week he was all for living in denial. Or maybe a better way to look at it—a healthier way—would be to call it *living in the moment*.

He and Sydney were in a good place. Since toasting her winning the interview, they made love with such frequency he thought he'd be physically depleted, but somehow he just wanted more. The two of them had spent every night together and they hadn't spoken a word about the clock that was ticking away the minutes until she would get on the plane that would carry her across the ocean to an event that could decide the fate of their future together.

Or so it might seem. The more time Miles spent with her, the more he realized that even if she went to St. Michel—and there was a good possibility that she would—he didn't have to let the distance dictate whether or not that would end their relationship.

He'd already decided that it wouldn't. He hadn't told Sydney about his decision yet. That would come in good time. This morning they were filming Lily, the weight-watching, pastry-baking schoolteacher, who had captivated the television viewing audience and won the contest. She was *Celebration's Bride,* and they were filming her at her final fitting of her bargain dream dress.

Sydney had gone on ahead to prep the bridal salon, whose owner had welcomed the shoot as free publicity, and talk a nervous Lily through the paces.

Lily had only been on camera one other time—when they had introduced her as the winner of the contest. She'd been a natural on camera. She'd been a little talk-ative, but that was better than a stoic bride and thanks to the beauty of editing, they were able to make the young woman look just as lovely as Sydney insisted they make her look.

"Just be true to her essence," Sydney had said. Miles was almost certain he understood. To him that trans-lated into *don't make her look bad on camera. Don't embarrass her.*

Sydney was protective of Lily. It took everything Miles had not to point out to Sydney that if she could be this caring for a virtual stranger, she'd make a fab-ulous godmother to her best friend's baby. But things were going so well between them he thought he'd let

A.J. be the one to bring that to her friend's attention, if she noticed it.

Right now—in this moment—Miles was guarding his time with Sydney and didn't want to ruin a good thing. He knew he was being selfish. He would cue A.J. in if he had to—if she didn't pick up on it first.

All in good time.

The bridal shop was in downtown Celebration. Miles found a spot along the curb and parallel parked his car.

The van that the camera crew used had scored a space in front of the shop and one of the production assistants, Jim, was running from the van back to the store with a reflector as Miles walked up.

"Hey, Jim, how's it going? Everything ready?"

"I'm glad you're here. You might want to come inside quickly. We have a *situation,* and Lenny wants to get it on camera."

"What's going on?" Miles asked.

Jim motioned him inside. "Come in and see for yourself."

When he stepped inside, the first person he saw was Sydney standing with folded arms talking—or more like listening—to Lenny, who was gesturing very animatedly about something.

"Miles!" Sydney walked away from Lenny, who was in midsentence. "Thank goodness you're here. I need to talk to you."

She turned to Dan, the cameraman, and said, "Please do not start shooting until Miles gives you the word. Even if Lenny says so." She shot Lenny a look of death.

"I won't shoot without the director, Sydney," said Dan. "No worries there."

"Thank you, Dan," she said. "I appreciate your willingness to be a team player. This is a very sensitive subject matter."

"What is going on?" Miles repeated.

She frowned and grabbed Miles's arm and directed him outside.

Once the door had closed behind them and they had walked away from the storefront windows to a more private spot, she said, "Lily's dress doesn't fit."

"What?" Miles asked.

"The dress that she's been working so hard to lose weight to fit into? It doesn't fit. The seamstress asked Lily if she'd gained weight and she fell to pieces. She's begging me not to put it on camera, and, of course, Lenny is foaming at the mouth to get in the dressing room with her and record every sob and tear in extreme close-up. I don't care how much money the man has, he has no decency."

Miles weighed his words. "I know you're not going to like what I have to say and you're going to think I'm just as heartless as Lenny, but, Syd, this is reality TV. This is what Lily signed up for. The audience wants to see everything that happens to the bride leading up to the wedding."

He edited himself and didn't remind her that Lily was getting a *free* wedding and a cash prize in exchange for letting the show film and air her story.

Sydney collapsed into him and his arms went around

her, a protective gesture that was becoming all too familiar.

"This is why I want to leave the show," she said, in a sudden twist of reasoning that he was trying very hard to follow. "I'm a PR person. I make my clients look good. I don't air their dirty laundry and failed diets. I can't in good conscience go in there and tell that young woman she has to humiliate herself in front of hundreds of thousands of people."

He steeled himself to say the words he didn't want to say, "But, babe, that's what she signed up for."

"I know she did and so did I when I agreed to be on this show. But I hate it, Miles. I am a behind-the-scenes kind of person. I can handle talking to the media to give them the information they need to get a story right, but I can't abide hurting someone."

Miles blew out a breath he'd been holding. The professional in him knew they had a crisis that needed to be fixed, and fast, but the personal side of him felt as if he'd been handed a treasure map. Or at least a huge missing piece of the puzzle that was this complicated woman who he was falling in love with.

Maybe it wasn't so much that she *had* to leave because it was time to move on, but that she simply hated being thrust into the public eye in a way that made herself and others look bad. In his business, he'd met a lot of people who would sell their soul for five minutes of fame, yet here was a woman who valued her privacy and integrity—and respected that of others—above all else.

That revelation unlocked the piece of his heart that

had been in reserve and in that moment, it became whole and completely Sydney's.

"Don't worry," he said, pulling her close. "We'll figure something out."

As he held her, she tilted her chin up and he met her lips with a hunger for her that couldn't be satisfied.

"There you are—oh! Oh, my. I'm sorry, I didn't mean to interrupt."

They broke apart and Miles turned to see his mother and Lucy standing there staring with looks of surprised elation on their faces.

"We heard you all were shooting downtown," Lucy said. "We decided to come down and check it out. Maybe they should bring the cameras out here. This seems to be where the juicy story is."

"Lucy!" Deena reprimanded. "You need to mind your own business and mind your manners. I'm sorry, Sydney, dear. Lucy is just a little full of herself today."

"I'm not," the girl argued. "They kind of made their romance my business when they decided to make out right here in the open in front of everyone."

A nervous hiccup of a laugh escaped Sydney's lips and she covered her mouth with her hand.

"Lucy, really?" Miles narrowed his eyes at her.

"Yes, Miles. Really. When are you going to tell me whether you'll come speak to my class? The deadline for signing you up is tomorrow."

"I told you I would if you're allowed to bring two guests. If not, you need to bring Dad. He has his heart set on this."

"Miles is right, Lucy," Deena said. "Your father has

been planning his speech for weeks. You know, you sort of did invite him when you mentioned it to him last month."

"I *did not* invite Dad." Lucy stamped her foot. "And I can only bring one person. I don't want Dad to come. No one wants to be pressured into joining the army. They want to meet you, Miles. They want to hear about your movies and all the stars you've met."

"Well, I'm sorry, Lucy," he said. "I can't make it. It's not that I don't want to come, but you asked Dad first. That's the way it has to be. Look, we need to get back inside. We have to work to do."

Lucy snorted. Miles ignored her, biting back the temptation to tell her to stop acting like a spoiled brat.

"It was nice to see you both, Mrs. Mercer and Lucy," said Sydney. "I apologize for…" She gestured in the air with her hands. "I suppose that was a bit inappropriate for us to do that out here."

"Nonsense, dear," said Deena. "I think it's wonderful that Miles and you have found each other. I'm just sorry we interrupted you. But you know what? On second thought, you can make it up to us by coming to dinner tonight. It won't be the big gang. I'll just be Dad, Lucy and me. Please say you'll come. The last time you were there everything was so hectic we really didn't have the chance to get to know you. So, we'll expect you around seven."

Sydney shouldn't have gone to the Mercers' home for dinner. She knew it, but she went, anyway. She was battling a strange sort of compulsion—she knew she should put some distance between herself and Miles, but she couldn't bring herself to do it.

So despite the hectic day—they had finally convinced Lily to allow them to film her wedding dress debacle, with the silver lining that Celebration's Bridal would allow her to wear any dress she wanted in their shop—here she was.

Sydney had promised that she would ensure that they downplayed the fact that the original dress didn't fit and play up the part that the bridal shop was giving her the gift of wearing the dress of her dreams. Sydney even convinced Lenny and Aiden to give the shop owner some on-camera time to bestow the gift on Lily herself.

It was a win-win for everyone involved.

That win-win left Sydney exhausted and wanting nothing more than to sink into a hot tub with a glass of wine. And Miles.

But no, as penance for getting caught *making out* with Miles in front of his sister, mother and the entire town of Celebration, to hear Lucy tell the story, she had to go to dinner with his family.

Miles's mother was a sweetheart and his sister, well, she was a little challenging, but at least Lucy's temper wasn't directed at Sydney. She felt bad for Miles, but at the same time she was glad he wasn't caving to the girl's demand. Since relations were rocky with his father in the first place, even Sydney knew that something as small as usurping the coveted career-day spot would only add fuel to the fire of bad blood that already burned between them.

She was amazed at how Miles wasn't letting that

bad blood get in the way of his maintaining relations with his other family members. It wasn't keeping him from his childhood home or leaching any pleasure he derived from having dinner with his family. Despite the way he and his father had gotten into it the other night, all Miles would say about that was that his father had started in on him about *Past Midnight,* asking him if he was happy that he'd capitalized on his family's embarrassment. And Miles merely said, "What's done is done. I'm not going to rehash something that can't be changed."

He left Sydney wondering if he meant the movie couldn't be changed or the legend that seemed to plague his father couldn't be changed. But what didn't escape Sydney was despite how each man seemed to harbor resentment, neither one seemed to really avoid the other. Miles still went to the house, ate at his father's table; the elder Miles hadn't told his son he wasn't welcome. How much of that was by Deena's decree, Sydney did not know. It didn't matter, really, because she wasn't about to bring it up to her Miles—

Her Miles.

The thought both warmed her from the inside out and terrified her. If she knew what was best for her she'd stop thinking of him that way…as *her Miles.*

There was no need to dwell on it now, not while they were at his parents' house and she was helping his mother put dinner on the table. Besides, who could think or rationalize with Lucy starting up again about career day? The child was persistent. Sydney had to hand her that.

As Deena called everyone to the table, Miles and Lucy were deep in discussion. To Sydney's surprise, the girl seemed to be listening, rapt, to whatever it was Miles was saying. Her entire demeanor had changed from the haughty teenager who had stamped her foot earlier that day, demanding her own way.

Sydney wondered what he was saying, but then guessed it must be some Hollywood talk. But come to think about it, he didn't talk much about his life in California. He didn't name drop and he certainly never put on airs. Maybe he was pulling out the arsenals to get his sister in a good place so that they could have a nice dinner. It might get a little awkward if she started hounding Miles about career day in front of her father. Worse yet, if she started spouting some of the same stuff she'd been saying today—about not wanting her dad to come—it could get downright confrontational.

She said a silent prayer for a peaceful dinner and took her place at the table next to *her* Miles. An oil painting of a mountain scene graced one wall. To the right, above a traditional cherry-wood sideboard adorned with silver candlestick holders and a silk floral arrangement, hung a grouping of family photos. She picked out Miles's school picture instantly. Slightly faded now, it had probably been taken in about the third or fourth grade. Even back then, he had the same mischievous brown eyes and lopsided smile that tugged at her heart. If he fathered Miles Mercer V, that's what the boy would look like. The thought made her smile.

For tonight's dinner, they had taken the leaves out of the table that when set at full mast could seat twenty.

Tonight, it had been broken down to an intimate table for six, even though they were only using five places. Deena and the elder Miles were each at the heads of the table. Miles was at his mother's left, Lucy was at her right. That left Sydney at the elder Miles's right.

Deena was doing her best to keep up a polite level of conversation that wasn't so involved that it kept them from chewing their food or forced them to talk with their mouths full; basically she filled what could've been awkward silence.

She had just asked Sydney to fill them in on what they had been taping at the bridal salon.

"It was a closed set," Deena said. "So we didn't get to see what was going on. Although I suppose you have to close the set or you'd never get anything done with all the onlookers. So, what happened?"

Before Sydney could chew the bite of pot roast she'd put in her mouth and swallow it—

"Oh, I'm sorry, dear," Deena said. "There's nothing worse than someone asking a question just as you're taking a bite. You take your time. Chew your food. Answer when you're ready."

But Lucy changed the subject.

"*Umm,* Dad? How come you never told me you fought in Iraq before I was born? I never knew you got your ass shot!"

"Lucy Denise Mercer! You watch your language, young lady."

"Well, is it true? Isn't it, Dad? Did you almost die?"

All eyes swiveled to the elder Miles, who was staring at her with an expressionless face. He lowered his fork, which had been poised midair when Lucy first began her line of questioning. Now his forearms were braced on the table. His hands were clenched into tight fists.

"I mean, I know you said Miles got shot because he was dinking with the video camera when he should've been paying attention," Lucy said. "But I never knew about you getting hit."

"Where did you hear this?" was all her father said.

"Miles told me, *duhh.* Where else would I have heard it? No one bothers to tell me anything around here. Especially not the good stuff. So he said you're a hero. Like a real live war hero. Is that true? 'Cause if it is, I can't wait for you to tell everyone about it at career day. I mean, you got shot? Like, for real?"

The elder Miles's eyes cut over to his son's. They locked gazes for a solid ten seconds.

No one spoke.

Sydney steeled herself for…for what? World War III? She had no idea what would happen. She couldn't read the father's steely, expressionless face. And she lacked the experience with a real family to even guess how this would play out.

It felt like the times in the various foster families she'd stayed with when someone would start yelling or swinging and she would do her best to disappear.

Here she was, thirty-five years old and she still hadn't gotten over it. She still wanted to disappear. The only way she knew to cope when things got this tense was to…leave.

But then something unexpected happened. The

elder Miles broke the staring standoff and looked at his daughter. His face softened.

"He said I was a war hero, huh?"

Chapter Thirteen

As Miles drove to work the next morning, he was still surprised that Lucy didn't know the details of their father's military career.

Why the old man had kept it a secret was a mystery. Actually, it was pretty par for the course. The things his father should share he kept close to his chest, while he spewed unfiltered thoughts and caustic remarks liberally.

His father's approach had become such a standard since Miles had served in the military and then opted to go to college that Miles didn't even flinch anymore.

He'd come to terms with the fact that he and his father didn't—and probably never would—see eye to eye. They were two vastly different people and Miles understood that. He'd never been the type to futilely bang his head against the wall when it was going to accomplish nothing more than giving him a bad headache. So when his father had taken issue with Miles's choice to go to college and leave the military, Miles wasn't surprised his dad had found reason to blow their relationship sky high, especially after his movie was a success.

However, his father was so volatile, Miles had had no idea how he would react to him telling Lucy the details of his past. He was glad Lucy hadn't mentioned she'd asked Miles to career day. Since she seemed to be happy with her war-hero father coming to speak to her class, her asking Miles would remain this little secret.

As he steered his Jeep into the Celebrations, Inc., parking lot, he saw Sydney's car. He glanced at the dashboard clock, which glowed seven forty-five. He'd left her place after midnight and she was already at work. The first one there. Even with a job interview on the horizon, you couldn't doubt her integrity. Now that they'd made love, he hoped that she would be just as committed to him—even if she got the job in St. Michel.

By nine forty-five, Sydney had already put in a few hours of work. Now she was in the kitchen, helping Caroline set out cake samples for Lily and Josh to try. The couple was due in at ten o'clock and they were scheduled to start taping the segment at half past the hour.

Caroline had made mini versions of her specialties. The sample cakes, which were the size of a large cupcake, had developed a cult following since the show had aired. There was a four-week order backlog and

Caroline and her assistant were baking them as fast as time would allow.

As Sydney set out the perfectly crafted red velvet mini cake—Caroline's specialty—she guessed that it would be the couple's favorite.

It was a game she played with herself—when they had brides and grooms in for a tasting, she liked to try and guess which flavor they would choose.

Sydney had only met Lily's fiancé once, when she, Miles, Lenny and Aiden were choosing the three finalists. This would be the first time since Lily had been officially chosen the winner of *Celebration's Bride* that he would be on camera.

Still, even with the limited amount of time Sydney had seen them together, she said to Caroline, "I'll bet they choose the red velvet. They just seem like a red velvet couple to me."

That's the flavor Sydney would choose if she were the bride. Reflexively, her gaze searched the set until she located Miles, who was studying something on a clipboard with Aiden.

As if he felt her looking at him, he glanced up, held her gaze in that sexy way he had, and then flashed that crooked half smile. A luscious shiver of wanting ran through her. She smiled back at him, but she hoped it made her look as if she wasn't affected by that smile… those eyes.

Even though she was.

Oh, she most undeniably was.

She looked back down at the cake, straightened the

plate and then glanced back at him, biting her bottom lip for effect.

Aiden must have said something that Miles missed because Aiden suddenly followed Miles's gaze to Sydney. When he saw what was going on, he rolled his eyes in mock exasperation. Then all three of them laughed.

Caroline came around the corner with a freshly frosted carrot cake. "What's so funny?" she asked.

"Aah, nothing…and everything," Sydney answered, her voice sounding a little breathless, even to her own ears.

It didn't take long for Caroline to catch on to what was happening. "God, are you two flirting *again?* If you weren't so perfect together, I'd tell you to get a room."

Her words stirred Sydney's fight-or-flight reflex, making it rear its head. It made Sydney take a mental step back. Why was she fine flirting and making love as if it didn't mean anything, but then when someone backed her into a corner and tried to hang a label on them—as a couple or being *perfect together*—she began to paddle backward to the distant shore of solitude and safety, where she could then run like hell.

She didn't look back at Miles. They both had work to do, anyway, since Lily and Josh would be here any minute. It felt a little late, so she pulled her phone out of her pocket and checked the time.

It was 10:05.

Clocks could be off five minutes in either direction, but she made a mental note to ask the couple to do their best to be punctual. Miles was making sure *Catering to*

Dallas ran a pretty tight ship and even a few minutes' delay could throw off the production schedule.

For an insurance policy, she decided to give them a call time fifteen minutes earlier than she actually needed them. That was a little trick she'd learned in her years of dealing with the media. That trick had saved her clients more often than she'd like to admit. And the vast majority were never the wiser.

She was just about ready to put her phone back in her pants pocket when it rang. Lily's number flashed on the screen.

"Please tell me you're not going to be terribly late," Sydney said in a cheery tone. "I just helped Caroline set out the most delicious cakes I've ever laid eyes on and I don't know how long I can keep from sticking my fingers in the icing."

There was a beat of silence that lasted a moment too long, and at first, Sydney was afraid the call had dropped. Then, in a rush of tears and sobs, Lily wailed, "We're not coming. Sydney, the wedding is off."

It was worse than Sydney had feared. When she'd dragged Miles to Lily's house, she'd gone with the intention of helping Lily and Josh quell prewedding jitters. Lily had said that Josh had called off the wedding because he thought she was making a circus out of it by putting it on television.

"He told me," Lily said between convulsive sobs, "that he wasn't going to be on television. I reminded him that this was the only way we could afford to have the wedding of our dreams. He told me it was the wedding of *my dreams,* not his. Then I told him, I'm only getting married once and I want to do it right in a way we'll always remember, and he accused me of letting the party get so out of control that it had become more important than our union."

Sydney wanted to bury her head in her hands, but she didn't. She sat ramrod straight with her hands on her lap on the same couch where she and Miles had sat two weeks ago when Lily had been all smiles, serving them coffee, tea and sweets.

Now this *Celebration's Bride* contest, which was supposed to have been a great way to reward a couple, to give back to the Celebration, Texas, community, had backfired and was threatening to tear this sweet couple apart.

The thing was that Sydney understood how Josh felt. Or at least she imagined she did. She wouldn't want to get married amidst the glare of a television production, under the scrutiny of a nation that was probably hoping something horrible, something just like this, would unfold right before their eyes.

This brilliant idea of hers had created a monster and if it was the last thing she did, she was going to make things right for this couple.

Lily and Josh had been together since they were teenagers. They'd made her believe in soul mates and happily ever after. Bloody hell, they were a bona fide unicorn couple.

Sydney got up and handed Lily a tissue.

"I have an idea," said Miles, who had been mostly silent as the ugly, tearful, heartbreaking scene had unfolded. He looked at Sydney. "I don't think Lenny is going to like it, but…" He shrugged.

"Who is Lenny?" Lily asked as a big tear meandered down her cheek.

"He's one of the producers of the show," Miles explained. "He likes to bring the drama, but I think we're going to overrule him this time."

He shot Sydney a knowing look and she gave him a nod of encouragement. She had no idea what he was going to say, but she wanted to trust him. At least he had an idea; she was coming with nothing.

"You are happy to be on the show?" he asked Lily.

She shrugged. "I didn't mind it when I thought Josh was okay with it. He said contests like that are a crap-shoot and he thought we'd never win. That's why he didn't object to me entering."

"How do you think Josh would feel if only you appeared on the show?" He paused, seemingly to gauge her reaction. "If he was okay with it, maybe he'd be okay with us airing a bit of footage from your wedding. Footage that your videographer shoots. We wouldn't come in there with our cameras blazing. That way you could still have the wedding of your dreams and we will still have the footage we need for the show."

Lily blinked and sat up a little straighter.

Of course! It was a brilliant plan and Sydney wanted to reach over and hug Miles for it.

Instead, she asked, "Do you think Josh would go for that?"

"He just might," Lily said, swiping at her tears.

"Well, why don't you dry your eyes and call him

and ask him to come over here?" Miles said. "Tell him that we've worked everything out and we want to talk to him."

Josh arrived about thirty minutes later. As he and Lily were having a private moment in the kitchen, Miles excused himself to go back to the set to deal with Lenny, who had called at least five times since they'd been there. Sydney and Miles had taken separate cars so that he could leave and get back to salvage some of the morning—possibly bump up one of the vignettes that had been scheduled for the afternoon in place of the thwarted late-morning shoot.

"He's probably climbing the walls," Miles said. "I texted him that we had a situation that needed tending to. I tried to keep it as vague as possible to buy us time to sort it out. Although I guess it was pretty obvious who it involved when everyone was missing when it came time to shoot this morning. I'll tell him we need to reschedule Lily for tomorrow and that you'll be back to shoot after lunch. Sound good?"

Sydney nodded. "He probably started rubbing his hands together in glee when he learned of this sudden shift in story line."

He planted a quick kiss on her lips. "Don't worry, okay? Everything is going to work out the way it's supposed to."

Sydney nodded, desperately wanting to believe him. After Miles shut the door behind him, the house was eerily still, except for the ticking of the grandfather clock that stood sentinel in the old-fashioned living room and the low murmur of Lily and Josh, who were still talking in the kitchen. Sydney had one ear trained on them to see if she could discern the tone of their conversation.

She didn't mean to eavesdrop or invade their privacy. She just wanted to be sure that they were going to be okay, that this television show hadn't torn apart an otherwise good relationship.

Sydney was due to leave for St. Michel in three days. Even though working as the press secretary to the royal family would bring its own set of challenges, at least she would be working for the betterment of something. The work she would be doing wouldn't be destructive. It certainly wouldn't be reality TV.

Suddenly, Lily let out a mournful plea and her sobs resumed.

"Oh, no." Sydney sighed. That did not sound good. She had to fix this, even if it meant releasing Lily from the show. The show could get one of the other runners-up to step in as the grand-prize winner. It's not as if it would be hard to find a taker. And next time they'd interview the groom more thoroughly to make sure he wasn't camera shy.

In the short amount of time Sydney had spent with Josh, he had seemed crazy about Lily. Unless Sydney had read all of the signals wrong. Had she been so blinded by the fact that the two had been together so long that she'd missed telltale signs? They had seemed so deeply in love, but Sydney had to wonder if she'd missed something.

"Josh, no!" Lily wailed as her fiancé strode into the

living room with a look of steely determination on his face. Lily had hold of his right hand, trying to pull him back.

"Please don't go," she begged. "We can work this out."

"There's nothing to work out, Lily," he said. "Stop embarrassing yourself any more than you already have."

Lily let go of Josh's hand, sank to her knees and covered her face with her hands. Sydney's heart was breaking as she watched the young woman fall apart.

"Josh, please," Sydney offered. "We can release Lily from the show if that will make a difference."

Josh turned his fiery eyes on Sydney, who reflexively stood up straighter, calling on every bit of her five-foot-nine inch frame.

"Nah," Josh said. "It's not the television show."

"Then what is it?" Lily yelled from her crouched position. "Tell me what it is, Josh. You at least owe me an explanation."

Josh turned around and smirked at Lily. "You really want to know?"

She nodded, mascara stains training down her cheek.

"You really want to do this here?" He gestured to Sydney.

Sydney considered offering to leave, except she really didn't want to leave Lily alone in the state she was in. The poor girl had lost her parents and her grandmother, and now her fiancé had one foot out the door. Sydney knew what it was like to feel so alone in the world that you had nowhere to turn, not a single shoulder to lean on. Unless Lily told her to get out, she was going to stay right here to make sure she was okay.

"You owe me an explanation, Josh." She was standing up now, looking rather formidable in her anger.

"You're too fat, Lily. I'm not going to marry you because you're too fat. You couldn't even fit into that dress you spent a house payment to buy. This is as good as it gets, Lily. You're just going to get fatter and the bills are going to keep piling higher. This is not how I want to spend the rest of my life."

Sydney stood frozen. If she didn't move, maybe they would forget she was there.

"Keep the ring," he said. "Sell it and use the money to make that house payment you spent on that dress you'll never wear."

With that, Josh turned and walked out the door.

Lily stood there for a moment as if she were frozen to the spot where she stood.

"Lily, I'm sorry. Is there anything I can do?"

Lily shook her head. "Just, please...leave. Please? I want to be alone. Please go. I'm...sorry."

The young woman turned and walked down a hallway. She disappeared into a room—a bedroom or a bathroom? Sydney wasn't sure.

She stood there for a moment, unsure what to do. Should she honor Lily's request and leave or should she wait and see if she needed her? It might be nice to have a friend at a time like this.

Only Sydney wasn't really her friend. She was the one who had gotten her into this ugly debacle.

As Sydney stood there stinging from the pain of Lily's humiliation, another emotion took over.

Wasn't this how it always worked?

Josh hadn't broken the engagement because Lily was too fat.

Lily's weight was simply an excuse for Josh's backing out of the wedding. He didn't want to marry Lily. Period. *Any* excuse would have done. It brought all sorts of unwelcome memories flooding back to Sydney. If someone made up their mind to ditch you, they would find a reason. Any reason.

Sydney had lived this nightmare more times than she could count on both hands—not with a fiancé, but with the various foster families who would take her in—some because they thought it would be nice to help a child, others because they wanted the small stipend that was supposed to cover her room and board. More often than not, in the end, it turned out that they couldn't keep her. She was too quiet…or too noisy…or too demanding…or too much trouble…or too much of a temptation for a husband with wandering hands and no moral compass.

Whatever the case, they'd always made it her fault.

She knew from experience it wouldn't be any consolation for Lily to hear that she was better off without the louse.

If it wasn't the weight, it would have been another excuse as to why it was her fault that things wouldn't work out. It was just so cruel to use her weight as the reason he couldn't marry her, because it so horribly undermined her self-respect. It would put the blame all on her, instead of Josh's being man enough to tell the truth—that he wanted out. That he didn't have the guts to man up and tell the truth.

The realization made Sydney's insides burn. And it just added fuel to the fire when she opened the front door to let herself out and saw Josh talking to of all people, Lenny.

Had this been a setup?

Had Lenny somehow gotten Josh to break up with Lily for the sake of a flipping reality-television show?

Suddenly, Sydney was seeing red and she let them both have a piece of her mind.

Chapter Fourteen

When Sydney didn't come back to work that afternoon, Miles went to find her. He'd heard firsthand from Lenny about how she'd flown off the handle at him and Josh, who, by the way, he hadn't paid off. Lenny had credited Sydney with coming up with a "damn good idea that he wished he would've thought of himself."

He had, however, gotten Sydney's tirade on tape and planned to use it and the footage they'd already shot of Lily to incorporate it into a new twist: *Celebration's Jilted Bride.*

Miles threatened to walk off the set, leaving them high and dry if Lenny did anything so tasteless. Something told him that now was probably not the best time to tell Sydney her performance had been captured for posterity, but he did want to make sure she was okay.

He stopped by Bistro St. Germaine and got a couple of sandwiches and an order of Bananas Foster. He hoped the offering of food would help her feel better and the Bananas Foster would take her back to that day when the two of them were so happy. He needed her to know that he was on her side.

"This is how things go in this business," he said. "Sometimes ideas work. Sometimes they don't. You just have to bounce back."

He had meant the comment to lighten the mood, but she was frowning.

"You're going to bounce back from this," he said, remembering that night of their first kiss in the kitchen.

"I know I will," she said. "But I don't want to bounce back to this. I don't want to do *Catering to Dallas* anymore. I'm just not cut out for that kind of career. Miles, if they offer me the job in St. Michel, I'm going to take it."

He sat back against the couch, letting all the air escape from his lungs upon impact.

"We're going to have to figure out how to make this work," he said, gesturing back and forth between the two of them. "Because you and I are too good together to let this get away."

He reached out and took her hand, but there was no life in it. Just her fingers lying limply in his hand.

She looked so vulnerable sitting there.

"I swear I'll never hurt you," he said.

She sighed. "You can't promise that. You don't know what's going to happen in the days or years to come. I still would like to believe that no one sets out with the intention of hurting anyone. But somehow things fall apart and it happens. Do you think Josh proposed to Lily with the intention of hurting her? No, but somewhere along the way things shifted and he did."

"We are not Josh and Lily," he said.

"I know we're not. But if I get that job, I still don't see how it can work for us."

"So, you're telling me you're willing to walk away?"

"When we started this, I told you if we got involved it would only be short-term," she said. "A fling. We agreed that's all it was. That's all it ever would be."

He couldn't answer her because the words were stuck in his throat, right there with his bleeding heart.

Sure. He'd agreed to a fling, but somewhere along the way he lost sight of that and had fallen in love with her. By sheer will, he found his voice.

"I may have said that, but things have turned out differently. I love you, Sydney. This is not just a fling for me. Never has been. Never will be."

Miles had told Sydney he loved her, and she'd said she needed space to think things over. She'd even taken the next two days off from work to claim that space.

Basically, she had said that she was leaving their relationship up to fate: if they were meant to be together the St. Michel job would fall through. If she got it... That would be the end of them.

He'd not gone more than twenty-four hours without talking to her since they'd met. It was a real test of everything he had inside him to not pick up the phone or, better yet, land on her doorstep. But he stood resolute, giving her the space she asked for.

To make good on that promise to her…or was it a promise to himself? He couldn't remember and really, it didn't make it any easier whichever way you looked at it. All he knew right now was that he didn't want to be alone.

So that night after work, he found himself at his parents' house. His mom had made her famous lasagna and had insisted he come for dinner.

"Bring Sydney," she'd insisted.

"She's out of town," he'd said.

That was all it took for the first round of fifty questions to begin.

"Listen, Mom," he'd said with all the love and respect he could muster. "I'll make a deal with you. I'll come over as long as you promise not to quiz me about Sydney. Deal?"

There had been a long pause and he was prepared for what came next. "Are you two fighting?"

"Mom."

"Okay. Okay. I promise. No questions. Just get yourself over here for dinner tonight."

She kept her promise. Mostly. If you didn't count the part where she informed Lucy and Dad to "Ix-nay on the ydney-Say." She drew her finger across her throat in what Miles guessed was a gesture that meant silence. Then she said in a loud stage whisper, "He doesn't want to talk about her." Then she waved her hands like a football referee calling a foul before busying herself in the kitchen, putting the finishing touches on the lasagna dinner.

Lucy was sitting at the coffee table in the family room doing homework. Miles had just walked up to see if he could help her when their father asked him to come into his den,

It was a strange sensation, getting this invitation from this man who had all but excommunicated him for the past five years. But Miles entered into his father's domain, unsure of whether he might be walking into friendly fire.

"Have a seat, son." His father gestured to the old brown plaid sofa that had been around for as far back as Miles could remember. The springs were sprung and the upholstery was way past showing its age, but there was something comforting in its sameness.

Miles sat down and stretched his arm across the back, feeling the nappy roughness of the fabric. Stretching his arm out like this made him think of how he'd gotten used to Sydney sitting next to him, how she seemed to fit just perfectly under his arm.

He felt like a part of him was missing without her here. He thought about calling her and dismissed the idea just as fast. Besides, his father was talking. He was saying something and holding a letter in his left hand.

"I know you and I haven't seen eye to eye over the past few years or so. I won't get into the hows and whys of it. You have your reasons for doing what you did, making that movie, and if you can live with it yourself, then I suppose I have no business judging you. I know you've been sending your mom money every month to put away for Lucy's college and I…well, I appreciate that."

He cleared his throat as if the thank-you had burned his esophagus.

"I'm glad I can do it."

His dad mumbled something under his breath that Miles didn't catch.

"What was that?" Miles asked.

His father frowned. "Your mother and I hate that we were never able to afford to send you kids to school. We never went. We couldn't do it for *all* of you. So we didn't pay for anybody. That's just the way it was." He punctuated the statement with a one-shoulder shrug.

"So I suppose that's why you did what you did, quitting the army—"

"Dad, I didn't quit. I proudly and willingly served my country for four years. Then I went to college. I may not have followed your mandate, but—"

"I know that!" his father shouted.

Miles held up both hands, signaling that he wasn't going to argue with him. He started to stand up and walk out, but his father said, "Sit down. I'm not finished here."

Miles hesitated, but decided to give the old man another shot at whatever it was he was trying to say.

"I…uh…I know I've never been supportive of your career choice, but…oh, hell, here, read this."

He thrust the white envelope he'd been holding toward Miles.

"What is this?" Miles asked.

"Do I have it read it to you? Didn't you learn how to do anything useful in college?"

Just ignore the barb. Don't fight back.

Miles studied the envelope. It was addressed to Sergeant First Class Miles Mercer. That was his father. Miles had been a newly promoted E-5 sergeant when he'd fulfilled his military service after four years.

He glanced up at his father.

"Open it," he said.

Miles picked up the envelope's flap and slid out the letter, which was written on plain, white-lined stationery.

Dear Sergeant First Class Mercer,

We are writing to you to express our profound thanks for the video footage you shot of our son, Brian. It was among his belongings that were returned to us after he died in Afghanistan. It was a true blessing that he called you a friend and had you by his side when he died. The gift of your video keeps his memory alive for us. That footage, snapshots and our memories are all we have left of him.

We will be forever grateful to you for your service to our country and for preserving his memory for us.

Bob and Patty Yeager, parents of Brian Yeager

It took Miles until he reached the end and Brian Yeager's name for the meaning of the letter to crystallize.

And then it took him another moment to reconcile the fact that his father was the one who handed it to him—

It had been addressed to his father by mistake. Probably because they were both named Miles Mercer…

Miles flipped the envelope over again and looked at the postmark. It had been delivered nine months ago. His father had held on to it for that long without forwarding it.

He wasn't going to fight about it with him. Whatever his reasoning for holding on to it, he was giving it to him now.

"Thank you for…" Miles looked down at the writing on the envelope at the name Yeager, written in bold black script, remembered his friend and said a silent prayer for him as the memories flooded back of that day when one soldier survived and another didn't. "Thanks for showing me this."

Miles stood to leave; this time his dad didn't stop him, but before he crossed the den's threshold, he did say, "I don't think you're a screwup. I'm proud of you for…your service."

Miles turned around. His gaze snared his father's. One corner of the old man's mouth tilted up in the closest thing to a smile that Miles had ever seen on his father's face.

Chapter Fifteen

Sydney got the job. The royal family of St. Michel wanted her to be their press agent. After working three days helping them prepare for the Royal Anniversary Celebration, running on very little sleep, she had emerged victorious.

She'd just come from the meeting where they had officially offered her the job. Her head was spinning as she stood under the palace portico waiting for the car to come around to pick her up, clutching a folio containing the papers that outlined the terms they'd offered. She looked at the leather case, ran her thumb over the smooth, cool grain embossed with the seal of St. Michel. Then she looked up at the grand golden mosaic design that adorned the portico's curved ceiling. The golden tiles shimmered even in the shadows of the curved archway. The handcrafted design on this private entryway had been there for centuries and represented everything that was refined and steadfast and stable. It had stood through generations, serving the Royal House of Founteneau well, withstanding storms and shifts in political climate. It would stand in all its finery for generations to come.

Sydney shifted the folio in her clammy hands, realizing that with this employment offer—a generous package that had been in Sydney's hands for less than fifteen minutes—she, too, could be etched into the Founteneau history.

For someone who had just been handed the chance of a lifetime, she didn't feel as elated as she thought she should. As a matter of fact, she couldn't get past the weighty residue of sadness and...regret?

She'd thrown her future up to fate: *I lose the St. Michel job, Miles and I have a future; I get the St. Michel job, my future is in St. Michel.*

Fate had spoken, and as she stood with the answer in her hands, she had to admit she didn't like the answer it had delivered.

On a sudden whim she decided that there was one thing that could trump fate: free will. She was nothing if not willful.

She waved to get the parking captain's attention. "I believe I'll walk back to my hotel rather than take the car. Would you please radio the driver and cancel it for me?"

The man bowed his consent. "Certainly, madam. Is everything okay?"

A lush, warm breeze swept through the portico. It carried with it the scent of jasmine and lilacs that had been washed by a Mediterranean sea breeze. She breathed in the perfume, hoping it would calm her. But it only made her heart beat faster.

"Yes, everything is fine," she said. "It's a lovely day, I'd prefer to walk."

"Very well," he said, his perfect English colored by a French accent. "Is there any other means in which I may serve you?"

"No. Thank you," she said. "Actually, on second thought, would you please point me in the best direction to leave the palace grounds?"

After all, most people didn't simply walk away from the Royal Palace of St. Michel. As she tucked the leather folio into her black patent quilted Chanel tote, the irony that she was doing just that didn't escape her.

The parking captain said something in French into his radio, presumably to the person at the next check point, and directed her to a cobblestone path running alongside the gently graded driveway that sloped downward toward the exit gate.

"Follow that path down to the guardhouse and they will let you out," said the parking captain. "Are you sure you would not prefer to ride? The car will be here in a moment."

"No, I'd really prefer to walk. Thank you, though."

The uniformed man escorted her to the cobblestone walkway and offered another bow. "Good day, madam."

Sydney nodded her thanks.

The lawn on either side of the path was lush, green

and manicured. Bunches of hydrangeas in vivid deep pink lined the way, providing a cheery, scenic decoration to the walk.

The palace grounds, with its grand spouting fountain in the center and display of sister-nation flags, painted a picture of ideal life. Actually, that's what St. Michel was best known for—the ideal life. It was a playground for the wealthy and famous. Because of the large amount of daytime tourist traffic, the high tariffs on lodging and money earned at the world-famous casino, the principality didn't need to impose an income tax on residents.

However, becoming a resident without a special "in" was next to impossible. The cost of owning a home in this postage-stamp-size nation was prohibitive and availability was almost nonexistent.

One of the perks that came with the royal press secretary position was a private apartment on the palace grounds. That was in addition to a car and generous salary. Of course, the flipside was that the press secretary was on call 24/7. So, her life would never be her own. Not on holidays or weekends. Theoretically time off was part of the employment package, but having the time to use the benefit was quite another matter. But the reason she was ideal for the job was she had the freedom of movement to commit herself to such an all-consuming responsibility. She didn't have anyone to worry about but herself.

Unless she did something to warrant her dismissal, she could be set for life.

Of course, a job like this would basically be sealing her fate as a single woman. Even if she was tempted to kid herself into believing that she would be in a position to meet heads of state and other dignitaries, as much as she would be working, there would be no time to nurture a relationship.

Miles's words about finding a way to make the relationship work echoed in her heart and gave it a little twist. There would be no time. Even if he would be amenable to moving here, in his business, the travel he would have to do to make his movies would render them living separate lives.

That was no way to live, even if he *did* love her… and she was beginning to realize she loved him, too. The thought made her inhale a sudden breath of air. She gave her head a resolute shake to rid herself of the petrifying thought.

After she passed through the guard station and was off the property and back on common soil, she turned around and gave the palace and its majestic grounds another look. The *Palais de St. Michel* was built in the thirteenth century. The exterior of the castle still resembled the original thirteenth-century fortress that was built to protect the principality of St. Michel, but the inside had been renovated and updated with the most modern of security and conveniences. It had 210 bedrooms and 75 bathrooms. Not to mention the 95 offices and staterooms. She'd learned all the facts about the place before her interview. If she would be representing the royal family and the government, she had to be intimately familiar with all the details.

One of the pieces that stuck with her was that the place was like a small city. It would be easy to get lost in there. A person could live or work there and never run into others who worked on the opposite end of the castle and never have need to leave the royal grounds, unless going out on official business.

The palace courtyard had been the setting for concerts given by the St. Michel National Orchestra, ballets by the national dance company and plays written by a state-sponsored thespian troop.

It was a country of people who loved and revered its royal family, and a royal family who took good care of its loyal citizens.

It was the holy grail for which she'd been searching all her adult life. Wasn't it? If so, why did she feel so ambivalent…and empty?

Miles's face flashed in her mind. She could see him with his little nieces hanging off him. He was such a patient man, such a good sport. She wondered what had happened with his father after Lucy had revealed that Miles was the one who had made her see that her father was a hero.

They hadn't talked since the night he'd told her he loved her. She'd half expected him to show up unexpected to take her to the airport the morning she left. When he hadn't, the disappointment she'd felt was real and raw.

But she'd told him to stay away. She'd said that even after he'd told her he loved her.

The thought formed a lump of emotion that lodged in her throat, making it hard to swallow, hard to breathe, hard to remember why she'd been so panicked.

It was easier to contemplate when there was an ocean

between them, easier to see that maybe, just maybe, the love that he'd offered so freely she had been taking for granted.

He loved her.

How could he love *her?*

Because he had a huge heart and an endless capacity to feel and forgive. Why could she not learn from him? Then again, could one learn to feel and forgive?

Especially when there was no one in your past left to forgive. Maybe she could start by forgiving her mother for dying and leaving her alone? Her father, whoever he was, for never being there in the first place? Herself, for letting her heart become so hard and weary?

She let each possibility resonate inside her, but it all felt hollow and empty. Exactly how she felt standing there contemplating these esoteric theories.

Maybe she needed professional help?

Or maybe she just needed to take this once-in-a-lifetime opportunity and not look back. A shrink would have her dredge up every past hurt and slight and examine it, wallow in it. What good would that do?

The hard truth was each person was dealt a different set of circumstances at birth. Some were born into better situations than others. Some had to work their backsides off for every break they ever got in life.

Sydney had never had patience for those who whined about their situation. She knew better than anyone that you made the best of what you had and worked hard to get where you wanted to go.

Well, here she was with everything she thought she'd ever wanted right in front of her.

Everything except Miles.

But where was it mandated that you were entitled to *everything* you wanted? No place she'd ever been.

She turned and headed toward the historic downtown area. It was in the opposite direction from her hotel, but that was okay. She was in the mood to walk.

It had been a while since she'd been to St. Michel. Her trip here last month hardly counted because it had been such a whirlwind. She wanted to soak it all in.

Her back was to the St. Michel Marina, where the rich and famous kept boats. Since property was so difficult to come by, sometimes people purchased boats and lived on them.

Downtown St. Michel was a gorgeous little medieval storybook village. Storefronts with hand-painted signs lined a cobblestone square, with narrow streets jutting into it like spokes on a wheel. She passed a butcher and a baker. The last time they were all there together, Sydney and her friends had joked about how they should open a candle shop next door so that they could be the candlestick makers and play out the age-old nursery rhyme.

Instead, they had opened a catering business.

Her heart twisted at the thought of not seeing her friends on a daily basis, not working with them. That would be one of the most difficult sacrifices she would face.

That, and possibly never seeing Miles again.

She needed to talk to Maya, who was really her closest friend. There would be a natural separation between Sydney and Queen Sophie. Even though Sophie had lived the majority of her life as a commoner and had been raised in the United States, decorum dictated that Sydney keep a respectful distance. The other people she knew in St. Michel were Margeaux and Henri Lejardin. Nurturing that friendship might be awkward since Sydney's unrequited crush on Henri had sent her packing to Celebration, Texas, when it became clear that Margeaux was the love of his life.

See how affairs of the heart have a way of messing up everything?

At least she had gotten some great friends out of the situation. A.J., Caroline and Pepper had gone to boarding school with Margeaux and had accompanied Margeaux back to St. Michel to make amends with her father before he passed away. Margeaux and Henri had reunited, and since Sydney had worked with Henri handling public relations for the state Department of Arts and Education, she'd had the good fortune of meeting A.J., Caroline and Pepper.

Pepper had even gotten her the job with Texas Star when it became clear that it was time for her to leave St. Michel. Now she counted the three women among her closest friends. And it was obviously mutual—after all, A.J. had even asked her to be her baby's godmother.

Oh, God! She'd left without giving her an answer. Maybe A.J. had changed her mind?

The downtown area was bustling. Summertime was prime tourist season in St. Michel. People were drawn to the island for its beaches and the famous yacht race held every August. This year the Royal Anniversary Celebration was compounding the crowds even more.

Sydney had to sidestep a family walking four abreast. The throng was so thick she couldn't even see the fountain, the centerpiece of the downtown shopping village. When she got to Maya's shop, there was a line out the door of people waiting to get in.

Well, good for Maya. It was great that business was so strong, Sydney thought as she did her best to shrug off the blue mood that was settling over her like a fine net.

She had always loved being alone and anonymous in a city of any size. It was easy to be alone in a crowd here in St. Michel. She had a sudden pang to talk to someone, anyone she could call a friend. Anyone with whom she could celebrate the coup of landing the press secretary job. Or maybe even just to hear a friendly, familiar voice.

On her way back to the hotel she called her friends. It was three thirty in St. Michel. That meant it was eight thirty in the morning in Celebration. Perfect timing. She could probably catch them before they began taping.

She went alphabetically so not to hurt anyone's feelings—*sheesh,* when was the last time she'd worried about hurt feelings? When was the first time, for that matter?

Right now?

The thought made her laugh to herself as she pictured her three girlfriends squabbling over who got the news first.

She got both A.J.'s and Caroline's voice mailboxes and left brief messages telling them she had *news,* but she didn't want to leave it on voice mail. "I'll call you again soon."

She dialed Pepper, who picked up on the first ring. "Sydney! Oh, my God, I'm so glad you called. We have a major situation here."

Sydney's smile faded.

"Hello, what's going on?"

"Well, apparently Lenny has some footage of you telling off that jackass Josh after he dumped Lily. Lenny is planning on using the footage and all the other tape we have of Lily leading up to your grand finale."

"What?" Her heart stopped for a beat and then kicked into a fast staccato. "I had no idea the cameras were rolling."

"Well, apparently they were," Pepper said. "I'm sorry to break the news to you like this, hon. That man is a monster. We have been up all night arguing with him. We're going to go on strike if he chooses to go with that angle."

"I screwed up in a big way by losing my cool," she said. "I'm so sorry. Did you talk to Miles about it? He won't stand for it."

"Umm, Miles isn't here. He went back to California the day after you left. I have a call in to him, but he hasn't called back yet. It's five thirty in the morning in California. It was the middle of the night when this started unfolding. But don't you worry. We have your back."

Sydney blinked at the phone. She had messed up in a big way by yelling at the groom. Her loss of control had put her friends in a bad position. Yet, they were standing by her. This had never happened before. No one had ever had her back when she'd messed up. That's when people always left. Or sent her packing.

"So Miles left, huh?" It didn't take him long to move on. He'd been out of there before her plane had even landed in St. Michel. Something empty and hollow cracked open in the space where her heart used to live.

"Yeah, he had some sort of a movie offer and he had to hightail it out of here. I don't know about that, but there's more that I need to tell you. I haven't even told you the worst of it," Pepper said.

Sydney stopped walking and a woman ran smack into the back of her. The older woman muttered something in French that Sydney didn't quite catch, but she wasn't really listening and she didn't really care. What she cared about was what could be worse than Lenny turning the show into a living nightmare and Miles hightailing it back to California.

"What else, Pepper?"

"A.J. has gone into labor."

"Oh, no. No! This can't be happening, she's two weeks early. She and Shane haven't even finished Lamaze classes. Please tell me she and the baby are okay."

"I'm at the hospital now and we're waiting. Shane's in there with her. So that's all good."

"Well, good. I'm glad to hear that. But, Pepper, tell me the truth. Did all this turmoil with Lenny send her into labor?"

"It's hard to say, hon. She was fighting with him pretty hard. Then when the contractions started the son of a b wanted the cameras to follow her to the hospital. Right into the delivery room. Can you believe that?"

Yes, she could believe it.

"I just about decked him," Pepper said. "But you know Shane, he wasn't about to let him in. So you try not to worry because there's really nothing you can do all the way over there in St. Michel— Oh, my gosh! I didn't even ask you about the job. How is everything going? Any news with it?"

"Actually, I got the job."

Despite everything, Pepper made all the appropriate noises, said all the right things that friends say when they're genuinely happy for each other.

"All the more reason for you not to worry about things. I will keep you posted. I'm sure everything will be fine with the baby. We have to think positive. Actually, that's all even I can do right about now."

"I'll be there soon to keep you company. I'll be on the next flight out of here today. I have to come home anyway to pack up everything. You tell A.J. and Shane that their baby's godmother will be there just as soon as she can."

Chapter Sixteen

It was the longest plane ride in the history of plane rides. All Sydney could do was close her eyes and try to push aside nightmares of anything bad happening to A.J.'s baby—her godbaby.

She listened to an audiobook on her MP3 player to distract herself, trying not to blame herself for giving Lenny the opportunity to pull a stunt that would send A.J. into labor two weeks early.

Sydney kept an iron grip on her emotions. That was all that she could do. Letting go of her self-control before was what had caused this disaster. If she let her composure slip now, she knew she would fall apart.

Twelve very long hours later, Sydney took a cab from the Dallas/Fort Worth Airport and was standing in A.J.'s room in the maternity ward of Celebration Memorial Hospital.

She had a goddaughter. Somehow, she'd had a feeling A.J. was going to have a girl.

Kelcie Marie Harrison had come into the world weighing five and a half pounds and measuring twenty inches long. Even though she was tiny, she looked perfect and beautiful.

She was the most beautiful baby Sydney had ever set eyes on. Sydney was instantly smitten. It was possibly her first case of love at first sight.

Well, maybe the second case if she counted Miles. But he really shouldn't count since he was gone. She didn't want to think about him right now—even though her broken heart begged to differ. Kelcie was what mattered.

The doctors had called her a late preterm baby, meaning that even though she looked fully formed to the uneducated eye, her lungs might need a little bit of time to fully develop and she didn't have enough fat to keep her warm enough.

Because of that, the little sweetheart would have to spend about a week in the neonatal unit. A.J. walked up to Sydney as she peered at the baby through the neonatal nursery window.

"Isn't she beautiful?" A.J. mused.

"Only the most gorgeous baby ever to grace the planet," Sydney said.

"Congratulations on getting the St. Michel job," A.J. said. "Pepper told us. You know how she is. She can't keep a secret, and I'm glad she didn't. Thank you for coming back on such short notice."

"Are you kidding? I wouldn't have it any other way."

Except if I could take back the stupid stunt I pulled when Lenny filmed me lashing out at Josh.

"I wish I could hold her," A.J. said. "I wish I could take her home with me this afternoon."

A knot formed in Sydney's stomach and she felt moisture pooling in her eyes.

"A.J., did the confrontation with Lenny send you into labor? I've felt so terribly guilty about it. I had no idea Lenny recorded me. If this is my fault, I just don't know how I will ever be able to forgive myself."

"Oh, honey." A.J. pulled Sydney into a hug and all the tears and emotion that had been bottled up spilled out. "No, the doctor said it was just one of those things. I had been feeling twinges even before we went head-to-head with Captain Exploitation. This was not your fault."

A.J. reached up and wiped away Sydney's tears.

"Look at me," Sydney said. "I'm a mess. You just gave birth and here you are taking care of me. For heaven's sake. What kind of a godmother will I be for Kelcie? She'll end up taking care of me."

A.J. beamed. "Does that mean you'll do it? You're saying yes to being her godmother?"

"I said yes a long time ago. I just forgot to tell you."

The two laughed and hugged again.

Over A.J.'s shoulder, Sydney saw Miles round the corner.

* * *

He had never met a woman who made him feel the way that Sydney James made him feel. He didn't care if he had to make monthly trips across the Atlantic to see her. He'd just make sure he had a good frequent-flyer program.

Pepper had told Aiden the news that Sydney had gotten the job in St. Michel. Aiden, in turn, had shared it with Miles, and he let him know that she was on her way back to be with A.J., Shane and the baby.

He'd wrapped up his business as fast as he could and had gotten on a plane with the hopes of seeing her before she left again, before he lost the love of his life.

He'd already decided he wasn't going down without a valiant fight.

He greeted her with a hug and paid his respects to baby Kelcie, who was a cute kid for being a preemie. In fact, Miles couldn't see a thing wrong with her. But apparently the doctors wanted to make sure she was in tip-top shape before sending her out into the world.

He didn't blame A.J. and Shane for being protective. Hell, he was going to be the same way when he had kids someday.

When Sydney offered to go get the proud new parents some *real* coffee, and not the dirty dishwater that the nurses' station was trying to pass off as Joe, Miles followed her out into the hall.

"I'll help you carry it," he said.

"Thanks. I need all the help I can get."

They both laughed at her lame joke.

For the first time in what felt like an eternity, he was

alone with her. He hadn't realized it until now, but his world had been slightly off-kilter since she'd been gone. Actually, since that night that he'd uttered those three words that had sent her running and he hadn't had the good sense to go after her.

Until now.

He knew that if he had to wait an eternity for her to trust him enough to love him in return, he would wait. Because there was no other woman in the world for him.

"I'm surprised to see you," she said. "I mean, I'm really happy to see you, but surprised. I heard you got an offer to direct a movie, huh?"

"Yes, it's another horror film. A big, gory commercial deal. The kind of film I hope my children will never see. Those movies damage your soul."

She nodded, but wouldn't look at him. "So, when does filming start?"

"I have no idea."

She slanted him a questioning look. "Shouldn't you find out? You're sort of an important person in the process. You should probably put the key dates on your calendar."

He loved her dry sense of humor. He loved the way her left eyebrow jutted up when she was making a point. He loved…hell, he loved everything about her. And he loved messing with her, too.

"Nah, I don't think so. I don't really care."

He made a *meh* sound of complacency and had to fight a smile when she pulled a horror-struck look.

"I turned the movie down."

"What? Really? How come?"

"I got a better job," he said.

She stopped and turned to face him. "Doing what?"

"There's a reality television show that hired me on as the permanent director and executive producer."

Again the incredulous look returned to her face. "And might I be familiar with this reality show?"

"I think you just might be."

She clapped her hands. "Really, Miles? Are you coming on permanently with *Catering to Dallas?*"

"I am."

She launched herself at him and threw her arms around him. "Everyone is going to be so happy. But what about Bill? Is he not coming back?"

"No, he has decided to take an extended leave of absence. Or at least that's the official word. The real scoop is that he couldn't work another minute with Lenny Norton. Truthfully, I think he's just burnt out."

"Yes, reality television will do that to a person. So will Lenny. At least you'll be here to keep the bugger in check. I'm still not so sure this latest stunt he pulled isn't what sent A.J. into premature labor."

"Neither were the big wigs at the Epicurean Travel Channel. They cut him loose. Said pushing the limits for reality was one thing, but his lack of judgment had become a liability. So Lenny is gone. But don't tell anyone. The powers that be want to announce it themselves."

The look on her face was priceless. He wanted to remember her that way always. While she was in St. Michel and he was here. At least he wouldn't be in California and have to travel all the way across the U.S. and the ocean to see her. It made flying from Texas seem like he was simply jumping a puddle. Hell, he'd swim the Atlantic if that's what it took to get to her.

There was the minor detail of convincing her that what they had was worth it. That they'd eventually find a way to be together on a daily basis, but he wasn't about to ask her to sacrifice this great opportunity. For now, he would find a way to make it work.

"I understand that congratulations are in order for you, too," he said. "I heard you got the job."

"Boy, good news travels fast, doesn't it? But thank you, yes, they did offer it to me."

"It sounds like a great opportunity. As the new executive producer, I'll make it one of my first projects to get Epicurean to release you from your contract. When do you start?"

"I don't. I turned it down because I already have a great job with Celebrations, Inc., Catering and *Catering to Dallas*. Fifteen minutes of fame doesn't last long. I'd better bask in it while my clock is still ticking."

"And here I thought you were the camera-shy one on the show," he said.

"Oh, I still am. There's another reason I've decided to turn down the job in St. Michel. I've realized I don't want a long-distance relationship. I don't want to spend another day away from you."

He pulled her into his arms and kissed her slowly and sweetly.

"I love you, Miles."

The following June, Sydney stood facing Miles underneath the ivy and flower-covered gazebo in the park in downtown Celebration. A.J.'s husband, Shane, looking sharp in his military dress uniform had walked her down the white runner that stretched from the sidewalk to the steps of the gazebo.

When the minister asked, "Who gives this woman in marriage?" Shane had said a resolute, "Her family and I do."

The words made Sydney's breath catch. She took a moment to gaze out at everyone who had gathered for the happiest day of her life. They *were* her family. And she was the luckiest woman in the world to have them all in her life.

How many people could say they were able to choose their family?

Then Shane lifted the blusher on her veil and planted a brotherly kiss on her cheek before joining A.J.'s sisters, who were caring for a healthy and thriving baby Kelcie, while he did his duty giving away Sydney and A.J. served as matron of honor.

She handed her bouquet of baby-pink roses to A.J., while bridesmaids Pepper, Caroline and Lucy straightened the train of her dress so that it fanned out perfectly, showing off the flair of the mermaid silhouette of her gown.

Miles's father stood next to him as best man. His brother and Aiden served as groomsmen.

She heard a sniffle in the front row and saw Deena, who had promised her that today she was serving as both mother of the groom and of the bride, brushing away a tear. She put a hand over her heart and blew Sydney a kiss.

With that, Sydney turned to her husband-to-be.

As Miles reached out and took her hands, she looked into his brown eyes and made herself think about what she was doing: she was about to vow to spend the rest of her life with this man—for richer or poorer; in good times and in bad.

The familiar troop of stomach butterflies were present and accounted for, flying in special wedding-day formation. It was the best feeling Sydney could imagine.

Miles was the love of her life.

She was *getting married*.

Settling down.

For the first time in her life, the only place she wanted to run was into the arms of the handsome man standing in front of her.

It was not only right, it was what she'd been searching for her entire life. She knew she'd recognize what she was looking for when she finally found it.

Without a shadow of a doubt, she knew Miles was it. There was no place in the world that she would rather be than right here, proclaiming her love for him in front of God and the entire world.

* * * * *

REQUEST YOUR FREE BOOKS!
2 FREE NOVELS PLUS 2 FREE GIFTS!

⊞ HARLEQUIN®

SPECIAL EDITION
Life, Love & Family

YES! Please send me 2 FREE Harlequin® Special Edition novels and my 2 FREE gifts (gifts are worth about $10). After receiving them, if I don't wish to receive any more books, I can return the shipping statement marked "cancel." If I don't cancel, I will receive 6 brand-new novels every month and be billed just $4.74 per book in the U.S. or $5.24 per book in Canada. That's a savings of at least 14% off the cover price! It's quite a bargain! Shipping and handling is just 50¢ per book in the U.S. and 75¢ per book in Canada.* I understand that accepting the 2 free books and gifts places me under no obligation to buy anything. I can always return a shipment and cancel at any time. Even if I never buy another book, the two free books and gifts are mine to keep forever.

235/335 HDN F45Y

Name	(PLEASE PRINT)	
Address		Apt. #
City	State/Prov.	Zip/Postal Code

Signature (if under 18, a parent or guardian must sign)

Mail to the Harlequin® Reader Service:
IN U.S.A.: P.O. Box 1867, Buffalo, NY 14240-1867
IN CANADA: P.O. Box 609, Fort Erie, Ontario L2A 5X3

**Want to try two free books from another line?
Call 1-800-873-8635 or visit www.ReaderService.com.**

* Terms and prices subject to change without notice. Prices do not include applicable taxes. Sales tax applicable in N.Y. Canadian residents will be charged applicable taxes. Offer not valid in Quebec. This offer is limited to one order per household. Not valid for current subscribers to Harlequin Special Edition books. All orders subject to credit approval. Credit or debit balances in a customer's account(s) may be offset by any other outstanding balance owed by or to the customer. Please allow 4 to 6 weeks for delivery. Offer available while quantities last.

Your Privacy—The Harlequin® Reader Service is committed to protecting your privacy. Our Privacy Policy is available online at www.ReaderService.com or upon request from the Harlequin Reader Service.

We make a portion of our mailing list available to reputable third parties that offer products we believe may interest you. If you prefer that we not exchange your name with third parties, or if you wish to clarify or modify your communication preferences, please visit us at www.ReaderService.com/consumerchoice or write to us at Harlequin Reader Service Preference Service, P.O. Box 9062, Buffalo, NY 14269. Include your complete name and address.

HSE13R

SPECIAL EDITION

*Handsome carpenter Dean Pritchett comes to
Rust Creek Falls to help rebuild the town after the
Great Montana Flood and meets a younger woman with a
checkered past. Can Shelby Jenkins repair the damage to
this cowboy's heart?*

***

Shelby laid a hand on his arm. "Please, don't stop. I like listening to you."

"Yeah?"

She nodded, trying to erase the tingling sensation that danced from her palm to her elbow thanks to the warmth of his skin.

"My brothers and I have worked on projects together, but usually it's just me and whatever piece of furniture I'm working on."

"Solitary sounds good to me. My job is nothing but working with people. Sometimes that can be hard, too."

"Especially when those people aren't so nice?"

Shelby nodded, wrapping her arms around her bent knees as she stared out at the nearby creek.

Dean leaned closer, brushing back the hair that had fallen against her cheek, his thumb staying behind to move back and forth across her cheek.

Her breath caught, then vanished completely the moment he touched her. She was frozen in place, her arms locked around her knees, held captive by the simple press of his thumb.

He gently lifted her head while lowering his. The warmth of

HSEEXP0713

his breath floated across her skin, his green eyes darkening to a deep jade as he looked down at her.

Before their lips could meet, Shelby broke free.

Dropping her chin, she kept her gaze focused on the sliver of blanket between them as heat blazed across her cheeks.

Dean stilled for a moment, then eased away. "Okay. This is a bit awkward."

"I'm sorry." She closed her eyes, not wanting to see the disappointment, or worse, in his eyes as the apology rushed past her lips. "I haven't— It's been a long time since I've—"

"It's okay, Shelby. No worries. I'll wait."

She looked up and found nothing in his gaze but tenderness mixed with banked desire. "You will? Why?"

"Because when the time is right, kissing you is going to be so worth it."

***

We hope you enjoyed this sneak peek at
USA TODAY *bestselling author Christyne Butler's*
new Harlequin® Special Edition® book,
THE MAVERICK'S SUMMER LOVE,
the next installment in
MONTANA MAVERICKS:
RUST CREEK COWBOYS,
a brand-new six-book continuity
launching in July 2013!

SADDLE UP AND READ 'EM!

Looking for another great Western read? Check out these August reads from the HOME & FAMILY category!

THE LONG, HOT TEXAS SUMMER by Cathy Gillen Thacker
McCabe Homecoming
Harlequin American Romance

HOME TO THE COWBOY by Amanda Renee
Harlequin American Romance

HIS FOREVER VALENTINE by Marie Ferrarella
Forever, Texas
Harlequin American Romance

THE MAVERICK'S SUMMER LOVE by Christyne Butler
Montana Mavericks
Harlequin Special Edition

Look for these great Western reads AND MORE available wherever books are sold or visit **www.Harlequin.com/Westerns**

SPECIAL EDITION

Life, Love and Family

Be sure to check out the first book in this year's
THE MOMMY CLUB miniseries
by bestselling author Karen Rose Smith.

When photojournalist Jase Cramer was injured in
an attack at a refugee camp in Africa and returned
home to Raintree Vineyard, Sara Stevens, his physical
therapist, gave him back his life. Now that a fire has
destroyed her home, Jase wants to do the same for
her and her four-year-old daughter, Amy, by inviting
them to live in the guest cottage at Raintree. But can
their sizzling chemistry overcome past hurts and lead
them to love again?

*Look for Jase and Sara's story next month from
Harlequin® Special Edition® wherever
books and ebooks are sold!*

HSE65759

SPECIAL EDITION

Life, Love and Family

Be sure to check out the third book in this year's
THE CAMDENS OF COLORADO miniseries
by bestselling author Victoria Pade.

Widow and grieving mother Heddy Hanrahan has
avoided relationships since the loss of her family.
So when successful businessman and single father
Lang Camden shows up on her doorstep offering
all the assistance necessary to take her business to
the next level, Heddy has no choice but to accept.
But will Lang's mischievous toddler drive a wedge
between them or bring them closer than ever?

*Look for **IT'S A BOY!** next month from
Harlequin® Special Edition® wherever
books and ebooks are sold!*